*An unusual marriage and unt
through a legal battle to save her*
In her seventh month of pregnancy, her husband becomes distant, foreshadowing the heartbreak to come. She struggles to maintain her physical and emotional stability until the birth of their baby. What follows is a drama-filled divorce as she fights to create a new life.

Praise for Sandra Walker's new novel The Seventh Month

The Seventh Month takes the reader back to the 1970s when women had few rights in love, marriage, and divorce. Abbie's dreams for happiness stop on the seventh month of pregnancy when she realizes her husband Sam is dumping the marriage, but separation means...she must live with Sam while he works...to destroy her. Abbie's struggles to hold onto her children and sanity are heartbreaking and inspirational. **—Janette Turner, Seattle, WA**

In *The Seventh Month*, author Sandra Walker skillfully guides us through the painful maze a woman experiences as she, seven months pregnant, learns her husband has decided he wants a divorce...The book tells the story of a courageous woman who must gather her strength to protect herself and her unborn child... You won't be able to put it down.—**Prudy Taylor Board, author, Murder a la Carte; Remembering Fort Myers**

I really loved this book. It was well written. It has warmth, truth, and the story about divorce will resonate with thousands of women.—**Susan Altschul, coordinator, Palm Isles Book Club, South Florida**

Sandra Walker writes a heartfelt tale that will keep readers turning pages until the end. Her heroine, Abbie Seligman, arrives in New York City a naïve, unpolished college student, drawn to the razzle-dazzle of the city. She meets a charming, young businessman and after a whirlwind romance, they are married. After years…her marriage goes seriously wrong. Walker's writing pulls the reader right into Abbie's struggles and triumphs. Intimate, compelling and heart-wrenching, The Seventh Month will keep you glued to every page, from beginning to end.—**Linda Rubinstein, cozy mystery writer, Delray Beach, FL**

A riveting story about a determined woman searching for a new identity. Highly recommend this book for a book club discussion.—**Sheila Seid, avid reader, South Florida**

A startling story of single life, dating, motherhood and divorce. Reads like a personal and beautiful novel. I was engaged and totally adsorbed. Written from the heart for every woman—**Susan Stuermer, retired teacher, Long Island, NY**

It grew late and the girls went to bed. Hour by hour, a sickening feeling grew in Abbie's belly. She called Sam's office repeatedly, but the phone just kept ringing. She heard his threatening words in her brain, "I'm tired of doing everything that other people want. I want to take care of myself for a change and do what makes me happy."

The thoughts in her head spun in circles. She tossed and turned all night and did not sleep for a minute. Sleep was impossible. By the time morning came, she ached miserably with fatigue and pregnancy hormones. Then at 7:30 a.m., the phone rang, breaking the numbing household silence.

"Hi, it's Sam. How are you doing?" Then too quickly, "I'm sorry I couldn't get home last night. There was something I had to do."

"Where were you? Why didn't you call?" Just silence until Sam cut the conversation short, saying softly, "I hope you have a lovely day." Then he hung up.

THE SEVENTH MONTH

Sandra Walker

Moonshine Cove Publishing, LLC

Abbeville, South Carolina U.S.A.
First Moonshine Cove Edition Jul 2020

ISBN: 978-1-945181-863
Library of Congress PCN: 2020910490
© Copyright 2020 by Sandra Walker

This book is a work of fiction. Names, characters, places and incidents are products of the author's imagination or are used fictitiously. Any resemblance to actual events, locales or persons, living or dead, is entirely coincidental.

All rights reserved. No part of this book may be reproduced in whole or in part without written permission from the publisher except by reviewers who may quote brief excerpts in connection with a review in a newspaper, magazine or electronic publication; nor may any part of this book be reproduced, stored in a retrieval system or transmitted in any form or by any means electronic, mechanical, photocopying, recording or any other means, without written permission from the publisher.

Cover photograph public domain; cover and interior design by Moonshine Cove staff

About the Author

Sandra Walker began her writing career as a reporter for local magazines in Westchester County, NY. She pursued a career in public relations writing articles and marketing communications. In 2008, she assumed a position as writer  and editor of *The Prepaid Press,* an industry trade paper. As self-publishing emerged, Sandra published three illustrated children's books in 2017 about the wacky adventures of Hilda "Ma" Tilda and her pets. All the while, Sandra worked on her novel until final completion in 2019. Currently, she is working on a second book about a single working mother and her struggle to juggle a career, love life, and a dominating ex-husband.

Sandra Walker is originally from the north side of Chicago. She is a graduate of Columbia University Teachers College and now lives in South Florida. The Seventh Month is her first novel.

http://sandrawalkerbooks.com

The Seventh Month

Chapter One
December 1974

The house on Spruce Lane in Pleasantville was much too lavish for a young couple in their twenties. There were elegant finishes and stylish furnishings in every room, meticulously arranged by a New York City decorator, well-known among celebrities and affluent executives. Still, children's laughter and antics made it warm and cozy, and livable.

It took a few years for Abbie Cooperman to get used to suburbia. Now that she was settled in, she hated to leave her young daughters even for one night to celebrate her anniversary with Sam in the city.

She could hear her daughters, seven-year-old Eve and five-year-old Lila, chasing each other around the billiard table in the downstairs recreation room. Abbie called out to them.

"What do you think, girls? Does this red sweater look okay with these black pants?"

"Yes, Mommy," said Eve. She came running, bouncing up and down on the king-size bed covered in aqua and pink. Lila was standing in the hallway waiting for her sister.

Outside, it was bitterly cold. The weatherman predicted a snowstorm for that afternoon.

"Come on, girls," said Ginger, the housekeeper. "Your mother has a train to catch. Put on your jackets and hats and let's go outside before it snows."

"Missus, you have a nice stay."

"Thank you, Ginger."

Abbie kissed each of the girls and hugged them. They squeezed their mommy tightly as she put on her wool coat and cashmere scarf.

"I will see you tomorrow. Daddy and I will be home for lunch."

"Have a good time, Mommy," Eve said, her blonde curls bouncing. "Tell Daddy he has to take us to see Santa Claus this weekend."

Eve was so fair and blonde when she was born that Sam's parents didn't believe their son could be the father. His dark hair and tan complexion in contrast to Abbie's light brown auburn streaked waves and ivory skin was striking.

"Bye, girls," Abbie said once more, as she lowered the window of her Mercedes and drove away.

She turned up the main road to the village, surveying the plush green landscape of their charming town — the arrangement of well-built houses of brick or wood siding with long driveways and chimneys. It was picture perfect suburbia like on a Hollywood set. *It reminds me of a Doris Day movie that made married life in suburbia seem utterly romantic.*

At the station, she parked in the back lot and waited for the commuter train into Manhattan. She heard the whistle, right on schedule. It stopped slowly and she remembered to step carefully over the gap between the platform and the car.

She chose an empty row, placing her small overnight bag in the middle of the seat. As the train moved forward, Abbie gazed out the grimy window at the suburban lawns, followed a few miles later by boxy, ordinary brick apartment buildings, one after another, in the Bronx and into Harlem.

I grew up in a building like that on a main street across from a park. I played hopscotch with my friends on the sidewalk. Someone always had a bag of big colored chalk. At night the neighbors from the three-story brick building sat outside on folding chairs and talked while the kids caught fireflies in glass jars.

The ride into Manhattan was about 40 minutes, just long enough to relax a little, and even doze a few minutes before entering the tunnel into Grand Central Terminal at East 42nd Street.

She got her things ready to step off the train, thinking about Sam's office on Park Avenue. *I wonder if he's there or out making sales calls.* He would meet her at the hotel at 6 p.m.

As she walked from the station to the elegant Regency Hotel on Park Avenue and 61st Street, light snow began to fall. If she tired of walking, she would hail a taxi. Seven months of pregnancy had slowed her down, but this special day in the city promised pleasure and a ray of hope.

Abbie worried that Sam would be late for their anniversary dinner at her favorite French restaurant. The reservation was for 7 p.m., although her husband was rarely on time for occasions in his private life. She planned to spend the day shopping for a dress to hide her bulging stomach. She could feel the baby move, its tiny foot pushing into her side. Boy or girl she could only guess, but it was restless to be born.

As Abbie entered the dazzling hotel lobby, she felt as plain as a suburban matron and worried that the evening would disappoint her. Distracted by the opulent space with the vaulted hand painted ceiling and glittering chandeliers, her anxious mood began to subside. Lifting her delicate chin, she approached the marble and gilt registration desk, as tentatively as a young girl in a foreign land.

"Good morning, we reserved a suite for this evening, for Mr. and Mrs. Sam Cooperman," Abbie said to the greeter, a young man in a dark blue gabardine suit. "My husband will be arriving later today."

"Hello, Mrs. Cooperman. Welcome to the Regency Hotel." He smiled. "Are you planning to stay over the weekend?"

"Just this one night," said Abbie. "I hope it stops snowing."

After checking in with Sam's credit card, a bellman showed her to the elevator, trimmed in marble and brass. Carrying Abbie's overnight bag, he led her to a suite on the 14th floor.

"This is a lovely suite right here to the left," he said. "You have a beautiful view of Park Avenue looking south. You can see the Pan Am building."

A bottle of chilled champagne and a silver bowl of fresh fruit rested on the antique French style entry table.

"My name is George, if you need anything. Or feel free to call the front desk. I can come up or they will send a maid from housekeeping."

"Would you like me to open the drapes to let in the sun, what there is of it?"

"Thank you, please," said Abbie, handing him a tip as he left.

"Have a pleasant day," said the bellman as he was closing the door. "It is supposed to snow until late tonight."

Abbie surveyed the rich décor of the rooms, marked by artful gilt sconces, tailored sofas and armchairs, and luxurious bedding. Shades of pale blue and creamy white carpeting offset the striped cerise and gold wallpaper. A gray velvet loveseat beckoned. At the window, she had a full view of Park Avenue, resplendently lit in the afternoon sun, despite the falling snow. *I can't wait until Sam gets here. I hope he'll be in a good mood.*

In the spacious bedroom, a romantic canopy shadowed the plush king size bed adorned with fringed pillows atop a textured white coverlet. Though tempted to lie down for a nap, she was eager to go shopping at Bloomingdale's and hungry for lunch and a frozen yogurt in the cafe.

I'd better give my mother a quick call. Let her know I'm here. She went over to the ornate white rotary phone on the desk by the window and dialed for an outside line. After the dial tone came on, she called her parents' number in Chicago.

She heard the beep-beep of the phone line, and then she heard her mother's familiar voice.

"Hi, Mom. I'm in the city at a hotel. Sam and I are celebrating our anniversary. How are you and Daddy?"

"Fair. What can I say? It's nasty here, gray and cloudy. We may get some snow. How do you feel?" asked her mother. "We're worried about you."

Bessie Seligman always anticipated trouble for no reason at all.

"It's already snowing here," said Abbie. "But I'm going shopping anyway."

"What about Sam? Is he still acting strange?"

"I'm hoping things will go well tonight."

"Okay, honey. Just be your sweet self. The main thing is your health and the baby."

"Yes, I know. I need to stay strong for my baby. Say hi to Daddy for me. Love you." Then she hung up.

Abbie glanced in the mirror over the French provincial dresser. She put on her camel wool coat, checked her Gucci handbag to make sure she had her wallet and lipstick, and left the comfortable suite. She carried her rabbit fur earmuffs on her wrist, knowing she might need them as soon as she got into the frigid air.

In the lobby, she pushed her way through the heavy glass door. The snow was still coming down and sticking to the pavement. Abbie felt the slick flakes under her rubber soled boots. The tinkle of bells from the Salvation Army Santa Claus and the scent of roasting chestnuts cheered her.

The department store at 59th and Lexington Avenue was only a short walk from the hotel. Relieved to get inside from the cold, she avoided the crush of the holiday crowd and maneuvered her way to the dress department with thoughts of finding something right for her rounded body.

I'm not going to the maternity section. Not today. I would rather find a loose-fitting garment that makes me look less pregnant.

A saleswoman dressed in a black sweater and flair skirt approached her. "May I help you?" she asked, smiling.

"Maybe. I don't really want a maternity dress, so I'm looking for something a little full that will hide my middle," Abbie said. "Or make it less noticeable."

"I think we might have a few things. Right this way." The woman positioned some dresses on the rack. "What month are you in?"

"Seventh month," Abbie said. "I feel like a blimp."

Together, they found several high waisted dresses that might be flattering, and she settled into a fitting room.

The light wool blue dress was not exciting, but classic and loose fitting. Pulling it over her head, Abbie stared at herself in the full-length mirror. Her auburn hair was bobbed, the way Sam liked it. She wore a slight bang off to one side of her high forehead.

"I like your hair short," Sam had said. "It shows off your brown eyes and high cheekbones."

In the fitting room mirror, she cupped her belly. *My stomach looks so big. I don't know how I'm going to make it until my due date. I feel like I could pop next week.*

She thought of Sam's recent odd behavior. Had he acted this way when she was pregnant with the girls?

I can't remember. Only two and a half more months. The due date was March 4. *We'll get back on track after that. I hope.*

Not sure about the blue dress, Abbie pulled the cocoa colored dress over her head, trying not to mess her hair.

This shade of brown and the A-line looks good. The neckline is flattering and it's a nice length with high boots.

Following this through, she realized she was starving. Abbie purchased the dress and took the escalator upstairs to the store's famous café. She ordered a chicken salad sandwich with lettuce on rye bread. For dessert, she had a vanilla yogurt with walnuts. It was sweet with a tangy taste.

Having satisfied her hunger, Abbie wandered through the main floor stopping to try on hats and settled for a knit maroon hat that fit her head. Carrying her Bloomingdale's shopping bag, she strolled slowly back to the hotel, conscious of the slippery pavement. She passed a young man selling roasted chestnuts and a Salvation Army Santa Claus ringing a brass bell.

Traffic on Park Avenue was crazy as a winter carnival. People were walking hurriedly on the crowded sidewalks. The men were carrying briefcases, but many of the women were holding shopping bags with holiday designs.

When she reached the doors of the hotel, the bellman was holding it open for her to rush in, away from the snow. She was glad to make it safely back to the warm, luxurious suite. She dumped everything in a chair, collapsed on the bed, and instantly fell asleep on top of the coverlet.

When she woke, it was dark outside. She checked the clock and was horrified to see it was 6:25 p.m. Sam should have already arrived for their special evening. Abbie lay on the bed worrying about her marriage. Sam was always late, but tonight was an occasion.

I was lucky to get the dinner reservation. Sam's secretary was right about calling six weeks in advance.

She had not heard from her husband since morning, when they confirmed their meeting at the hotel.

He's always late, and difficult to reach, but tonight? It's inexcusable.

Abbie nervously dialed out on the hotel phone to call Sam's office. No one answered.

Waiting for Sam, the beautiful suite felt like a torture chamber. Why hadn't he called her to say he'd be late? Lately he never hugged or kissed her. He rarely checked up on her during the day. Today seemed like the longest day of all without a word from him. *What was the problem now?*

She stared out of the floor-to-ceiling window at glittering, busy Park Avenue, mesmerized by the oversized snowflakes against the ebony starlit night. Everywhere was covered with snow and slush, yet people were walking briskly, hurrying to their destinations, despite the slickness. Everyone was carrying packages or shopping bags. As hard as she stared, she couldn't make out the one form, the one person who could calm her. If she wasn't pregnant, she might have lit a cigarette, though she rarely smoked any more.

Pacing nervously, she took deep breaths and stared at the door, then looked out the windows again. She called her mother-in-law to ask casually if she had heard from Sam.

"It's such a terrible night," Sophia said. "I think it's a blizzard. Be careful. Make sure the restaurant stays open."

"I'm sure it will be. I just haven't heard from Sam and we have a 7 o'clock dinner reservation at Lutèce." She didn't want to overdramatize his tardiness. Maybe it was nothing.

She hung up with her mother-in-law and called the restaurant to hold the reservation.

Feeling the baby move inside her, she watched as a tiny limb pushed out her stomach. She took a deep breath, wondering when and if Sam would arrive.

Chapter Two

Waiting for Sam, Abbie recalled that many difficult experiences in her childhood had taught her to be cautious and watchful, to wait for the other shoe to drop. Like the time she skinned her knees roller skating. Humiliated, she had locked herself in the bathroom and cried. Or when her second-grade teacher asked her to explain "new" math and her mind went blank. Feeling confident seemed unattainable.

When Sam fell in love with her, it had been a dream come true for a plain, poor girl from the North side of Chicago. Not that Sam was wealthy, but he was ambitious and resourceful.

Moving to the rolling green suburbs not far from a sophisticated city was a sharp contrast to the walk-up apartment where she'd grown up in a modest Midwest neighborhood. She thought about her life in their rambling house where often she felt empty, alone, and friendless in the quiet lanes of suburbia.

The hotel suite had darkened, while Abbie's mind simmered with worry and doubt. It had been hours. *I got here about 12 noon, went shopping, had lunch, took a nap, and I'm still wondering and waiting. He is so inconsiderate.*

Her beautiful daughters kept her busy with school activities, ballet classes and play dates. Mothers in town would call each other and make appointments. But it wasn't enough.

Sam's endless business excursions left her alone, like a single parent. The trips usually were extended from the promised two weeks to three, then four, and many times five or six weeks before his work was finally accomplished.

Abbie's complaints amounted to frustrated pleas. Sympathetic friends who knew the couple said one way or another, "Sam has a passion and there's not much you can do about it."

"He does adore you. That is for sure," Carol said.

Regardless, Sam had become a part-time husband and father and when he arrived home, he behaved as if he were still far away.

Alone in the hotel suite, Abbie steeled herself for Sam's eventual arrival. *Where was he? Why was he so late?* Abbie's reverie was interrupted when she heard a knock on the door. Sam came rushing in, throwing off his wet wool overcoat, ranting about the latest business disaster.

Barefoot, she ran to embrace him and kissed him quickly on his cold, snow-bitten cheek.

"Hi, honey, what happened? Where have you been?" she said in a light tone, all the while frightened and cringing inside.

Another business catastrophe. The factory samples were delayed again, his salespeople were failing to meet their quotas, and lenders were behind with funds.

Then, "Happy anniversary." Sam gave her a quick peck on the cheek.

"Do you still want to go to Lutèce?" he asked.

"I do, I'm really hungry," she said, sensing his reluctance. She hurriedly put her black tights on under her new dress and slipped on her tan suede leather boots.

The weather grew so grim that the restaurant held their coveted reservation. Out on Park Avenue, they made their way cautiously through the drifts of snow. When they got near Fifth Avenue, Sam hailed a taxi.

Abbie's feet felt brutally frozen. She touched her stiff belly and felt the baby's strong kick.

On East 50th Street, Lutèce was famous for classic, fine dining. It had an avantgarde atmosphere with cushy dark red velvet upholstery and magical scenes of Paris framed in gold on the vividly painted walls. The scent of roses, both pink and red set on every table, permeated the air. Few diners were in attendance on this snowy night. The atmosphere was still, soft sounds of dishes being served were barely audible.

The maitré d in a black tuxedo greeted them warmly and showed them the way to a cozy banquette.

A waiter in a white shirt and silk vest quickly approached them, offering menus and a carafe of water.

"Good evening. Welcome. I'm glad you made it, considering the weather," the waiter said. "May I bring you a cocktail or wine? Or a bottle of Perrier?"

"Thank you. We didn't want to miss our reservation. Would you suggest a nice Chablis?" Sam asked. "Darling, what would you like?"

"I'll just have a white wine spritzer."

The waiter brought crisp French bread to the table and a plate of olive oil sprinkled with chopped basil.

The oversized menu featured a rose color and green engraving of a Rose pasted on the front. The menu choices for the evening were in calligraphy with no prices listed.

"Tonight, we are offering cote de boeuf. We also have sole meuniere, or sea bass," the waiter said. "I can highly recommend both."

"You may want to review the menu. There is also a lovely roasted salmon with a wine and caper sauce."

"By the way," said the waiter, "Our chef Andre Soltner is in the kitchen tonight and you can meet him later on."

"That would be lovely," Sam said. "It's our anniversary so we should mark the occasion. In fact, we should have some champagne."

Abbie surprised, said, "Yes, sweetheart, that would be nice."

After a few moments of thought, Sam ordered the filet of beef with potatoes and blanched green beans. Abbie could tell he was famished.

"I will have the sole with asparagus and rice pilaf," she said. "and a green salad with vinaigrette dressing."

Sam's mood had softened. The dishes arrived looking elegant and delicious. He was charming throughout dinner, bantering about business and asking about the girls.

Still, it had been a long day for both. Tortuous waiting.

Smiling, Abbie said, "Sweetheart, I know it's been a difficult day. But glad we made it to dinner here… and you know, they have incredible chocolate mousse."

After their satisfying meal, they ordered one to share.

"I feel better now that I have eaten. It's been a frustrating day," Sam said.

The chef appeared in a white apron. Graciously, he offered his gratitude.

"Thank you for coming out on such a wintry night. May we offer you a cognac before you step out into the snow?" he said. "I hope you don't have far to go."

Sam reacted with a smile. "We've had a long day, but we didn't want to miss our anniversary dinner."

"Much happiness to you and your wife. I'll be right back."

In just a few minutes, the chef was back with two small crystal glasses on a tray.

Misty eyed Abbie said, "We used to have nights like this. I wish we could have them again."

Sam paid the bill with his credit card and they got up to leave. Chef Soltner helped Abbie put on her coat and scarf. Then he helped Sam with his black wool coat.

Abbie sighed as she put on her new hat.

It's too late and too cold to worry about how my hair looks.

Feeling exhausted by the weight of her middle, Abbie clinged to her husband's arm as they walked. She couldn't help seeing desperate passengers clinging with all their strength to a sinking ship.

The streets were completely white, covered in frosty snow, still falling from the gray sky. The sidewalks looked slick as an ice-skating rink. A few cars drove slowly down the side street near their hotel.

She glanced at Sam. *He's a tough man to know.* One minute he could be tender, the next serious and sullen. He once was a vigorous lover, but that was gone. He had been attentive, often adoring, until this third pregnancy, but now he had changed.

You're such a handsome and successful man. Charismatic, but complicated and sometimes thoughtless and uncaring."

"I had a wonderful evening. I hope we can have more." Abbie said.

She looked to him for a gesture, a word. Her hand on his tawny cheek, she kissed him where his dark beard made a shadow.

Years later, Abbie would recall that night. *Wet snowflakes fell on their youthful faces. It was a moment frozen in time.*

By now, she realized that all couples go through ups and downs, even fiery spats. *On our 50th anniversary, we will look back and laugh as we play with our grandchildren. Maybe this is just a singular episode in our lives. Maybe...*

Her mind replayed old memories.

Chapter Three
July - August 1965

I would have never met Sam Cooperman, if my first serious boyfriend had not gotten cold feet and broken my heart.

That man she fell in love with was a regular sporty guy with a big personality. They met at a bar in Manhattan when she was working at the World's Fair. Exciting things had happened that a callow girl from the Midwest never expected.

How crazy it was how she had gotten a job at the New York World's Fair as a hostess at the Illinois pavilion in the second summer of the fair.

Her mother, Bessie, had encouraged her to apply. "Do something different. Get away from here for a change."

Abbie told her best friend Roz, "I graduated from college and have a teaching job in Chicago, but it seems like there should be more. My parents don't even have room for me in their new apartment."

Abbie had been teaching in the Chicago public schools on the West side, driving back and forth an hour each way through congested streets. The kids in her first-grade class were unruly, beyond her control. They ran around the room chasing each other until one of the veteran teachers intervened with a wooden yardstick and threatened them to sit down in their seats.

Sometimes a teacher banged the desk, and even whacked an uncontrollable child, shaking Abbie's nerves. Her college training had not prepared her for teaching children on the impoverished West side. At the end of each day, she drove home and crawled into bed, pulling the blanket up to her chin.

After six months of depression, she went downtown to the Board of Education to request reassignment to another school. It was January, right after her birthday and the winter semester had begun. She went up to the first person she could find in the administration building.

It looks like the inside of a prison — dark and antiquated.

"Good morning, I'm a teacher doing my first assignment at the Lawson School." Breathless, Abbie wept. "I don't think I can take it anymore. What can I do?"

The clerk muttered, "What took you so long? Most of your classmates from college have already gotten transfers."

Abbie was reassigned as a substitute teacher in a middle-class neighborhood on the Northwest side. When she reported to work, the principal was eager to get her acclimated and soon a fifth-grade class became her responsibility on a temporary basis while their regular teacher was on maternity leave. It was Abbie's job until the end of June.

"Mom, I'm starting to think that teaching is not for me," Abbie said. "The kids I have now actually listen to me and do their work, but it's not even a permanent job."

"You're only 20 years old, almost 21. You have to think about what you really want to do, until you find a nice boy to marry," Bessie said.

Her mother's remark reminded Abbie that most of her friends already had diamond engagement rings and were planning their weddings.

I've never even had a serious boyfriend. I feel like a loser.

One Saturday afternoon, Abbie was helping her mother at home. The radio was playing "We Can Work it Out," a Beatles song, and the latest news was about the war in Viet Nam. President Lyndon Johnson was making a statement about the deployment of more servicemen.

Abbie was leafing through the local newspaper while her mother was in the kitchen preparing a meatloaf with chunky potatoes around the bottom of the pan. She sprinkled some tomato sauce on the top of the meat.

The family had recently moved to a nicer apartment building in a better section of their neighborhood, but they had taken a one-bedroom apartment. Abbie was sleeping on a sofa bed in the living room.

"Look at this ad for jobs at the World's Fair in New York City," Abbie said. "Do you think it's real?"

Bessie wiped her slippery hands on a red checkered dish towel and glanced over. "Hmmm, maybe. It's from a department of Illinois State. You should send an application. You have nothing to lose."

Before she could change her mind, Abbie composed a letter answering the ad, wrote a brief essay on why she wanted to represent her state, and inserted a pleasing school photograph of herself. The next morning, she mailed the package to Springfield, Illinois.

Abbie wrote in her diary: *I sent the application but why would they choose me out of thousands of people who apply?*

She thought about what she had been doing with her life and the opportunities that had been made available to her.

I have been lucky many times.

During her last year of college, she had been assigned as a student teacher at the Bell School for the Deaf, a public school with a special section for hearing impaired and blind children. Abbie volunteered to work extra hours assisting a master teacher named Mrs. Marlow.

A spunky lady who had once been an actress, Marjorie Marlow recognized Abbie's ambition.

"You know, Abbie, you might want to apply for a graduate degree in deaf education. There's a great program at Columbia University in New York City."

Abbie found out that the program offered a scholarship. Excited, she told Roz, "I've got two shots at getting out of Chicago. One chance is a job at the World's Fair and the other is a fellowship at Columbia."

"Why do you want to leave Chicago?" Roz questioned.

The friends were born-and-bred North side girls, best friends in high school. They were inseparable on weekends, unless one had a date.

Roz was a cute, perky blonde who easily attracted boys with her easy banter. Abbie's appearance verged on prettiness, but she was quiet and reserved. She attracted studious men who liked slim girls with auburn hair and fawn colored eyes.

"You are my most important tie to Chicago. I'm scared to leave, but I feel displaced. My parents have such a small apartment now, there's hardly any room for me. I don't know where to go and have no steady job."

In late April, Abbie received a letter from the State of Illinois congratulating her on being selected to represent the Land of Lincoln pavilion at the World's Fair. The letter included a list of 19 young women and men, hosts and hostesses welcoming visitors and guiding them through the show.

"Mom, I can't believe this. I got a letter about the World's Fair job. Take a look!"

"We get uniforms and $600 for six weeks of work," said Abbie, jumping up and down. "They pay for a one-way airplane ticket."

The selection committee provided instructions about when to report to the New York City fair headquarters for orientation and training in early July. It was to be the last six weeks of the fair.

The fair had been open since April 1964 and would close in the fall of 1965. The newspapers had given it rave reviews, reporting that the 150 pavilions were the most exciting and original of any other exposition, especially the ingenious Walt Disney attractions.

The Illinois pavilion featured exhibits that told the story of the "Land of Lincoln" and introduced the audio-animatronic Abraham Lincoln, a life-like figure that rose from a high-backed chair to recite the stirring Gettysburg Address.

That night, she and her friend Roz went to the local theater to see *Doctor Zhivago*.

"I have something to tell you. I'm so excited," Abbie said. "I got the job at the World's Fair and I'm going to take it."

"Abbie, that is incredible. I'm so happy for you," Roz said. Then she started to cry.

"I'm thrilled for you, but sad that you are leaving Chicago. Will you come back after the job is over? What about the graduate school scholarship?"

"Well, I qualified for the program, but all the spots are filled. They put me on a wait list," Abbie said.

"What's a wait list?"

"It means if someone cancels, I could get the fellowship."

"So, you might not come back. You might never come back home."

"I don't know. I'm getting scared about going to New York." Going to a place the size of New York was a frightening idea.

I might as well be going to the moon.

Weeks to go before she left Chicago, a plan emerged. Her mother had taken a phone call from one of the girls who was also going to work at the Illinois pavilion.

"Somebody called to say that you are to meet in Queens where you can all go look for an apartment together," said Bessie. "Oh, and there is a get together next week on the South side at someone's house. Her name is Penny."

Chapter Four

Penny Hirsch, a vivacious girl with freckles on her nose and a long honey-colored ponytail, welcomed her guests. She lived with her parents and younger brother in a stately brick colonial house on the South side of Chicago.

Jan Goldman from Springfield, Illinois was there, and so was Tony Kerner, the grandson of the governor of Illinois. The two knew each other from the state capital. Other pavilion hosts and hostesses who had been selected were from other towns in the state: Carbondale, Aurora, and Peoria.

Jan was a tall willowy blonde with light blue eyes and a perfectly turned up nose. She spoke with a refined downstate Illinois accent and moved like the debutantes that Abbie had seen on television shows.

Abbie and the other young women chatted excitedly about their hometowns, their colleges, and what they wanted to do in New York.

"What made you apply for this job?" Abbie asked.

Poised and confident, Jan tossed her blonde hair slightly and looked at Abbie with curiosity.

"I thought it would be fun. I love New York. My Uncle Al was on the state selection committee. Actually, he told me to get in touch with you."

"Really?" Abbie was too shy to ask more than that.

Jan, the eldest of three children, had been to New York often with her father, a successful businessman who was active in state politics.

On July 5, the six girls flew into LaGuardia Airport and met in the American Airlines terminal. As they deplaned, a woman in a blue uniform and a tall man in a suit were waiting with a sign that said, "Welcome, Hostesses of the State of Illinois World's Fair."

"Howdy," Jan said. The girls gathered together and went to pick up their baggage. The welcoming committee led them to a small private room at the airport where beverages and snacks were served.

"We have an apartment for you to see and if you like it, you all will live there during your stay at the fair. It's in a residential neighborhood only a few subway stops from the fairgrounds," said the representative. "There's a car that will take you to a real estate leasing office in Jackson Heights, Queens."

There they found out that temporary housing was scarce. "You'll be in a residential neighborhood close to the subway line," the agent explained. "There's a six-room apartment that could work for you girls."

"I have to warn you though. It's shabby, but there's furniture and you can clean up the place."

Jan said, "If there are three bedrooms, we'll take it." She was so wholesome, polite and demure, and a leader too. She immediately became the organizer of the group.

Abbie didn't know a thing about cleaning an apartment, except for dusting furniture. Jan, who lived in a mansion, knew exactly what to do with a broom, a mop and a pail of water. She set to work scrubbing floors and made their temporary home a livable place.

"The first thing I learned here was how a rich girl knew how to clean a house," Abbie told her friend Roz.

On their first day at the fair, the girls went through orientation. Abbie felt like a celebrity, still wondering how she had been chosen. The Illinois pavilion was considered one of the most popular attractions at the fair, showcasing an audio-animatronic Abraham Lincoln, the first robotic figure of its kind.

Every morning when the fair opened, long lines of people waited to get into the one-story, red brick building. Visitors entered though an exterior courtyard with softly curved walls, led by a welcoming hostess, reciting the history of Illinois, the prairie state where Lincoln came to reside and prosper. An exhibit hall featured enlarged photographs of the prairie state, its flat rural landscapes and its bustling urban areas in Chicago. Famous quotations from Lincoln lined the concrete block walls.

On the second day of training, the managers took the trainees by private van to Lord & Taylor department store on Fifth Avenue where they were fitted with white blouses, blue blazers and black pleated skirts, and one-inch black patent pumps.

"How are we going to memorize our lines in two days?" Jan said to the other girls.

"Welcome to the Illinois Pavilion, today you will hear Abraham Lincoln recite the Gettysburg Address....... Lincoln was the 16th president of the United States and served our country during the Civil War...... once you

leave the building, we invite you to drop by the prairie house behind the theater for some treasures from the Land of Lincoln."

The girls were busy memorizing their speeches and on the third day, Abbie nervously stood at the entry podium, welcoming the crowds that came to see and hear the high-tech audio-animatronic Abraham Lincoln. After the welcome speech, she led the crowd past the exhibits and into the huge theater. The state song resounded in the background,

"By thy rivers gently flowing, Illinois, Illinois, O'er thy prairies verdant growing, Illinois, Illinois...." The final verse made her tear up.

Not without thy wondrous story, Illinois, Illinois, Can be writ the nation's glory, Illinois, Illinois, On the record of thy years, Abraham Lincoln's name appears, Grant and Logan, and our tears, Illinois, Illinois, Grant and Logan, and our tears, Illinois.

When the theater was filled, a hush came over the audience of 500 visitors. All eyes were on Lincoln as he stood and stepped forward to a podium to address the visitors, who seemed gripped with emotion, almost in a state of bliss. Each time she watched the show, Abbie got goosebumps.

Abbie started to keep a diary and she wrote: *"The Gettysburg Address is the most meaningful speech on the definition of liberty. Amazingly, every word of it applies to current times. Everyone says it is marvelous."*

The summer was shaping up to be both marvelous and life-changing.

Chapter Five

Abbie's diary began to fill up with stories about her new job, her roommates, and her exhaustion from working and living in the scorching hot city.

She wasn't sure what she would find in New York, but she was open to exciting adventures, Broadway shows, Manhattan night life, and urban scenery. In her diary, she talked about finding love.

I know that a relationship can work if there is chemistry. So long as there are good intentions, you can work out problems. It is possible to marry and live happily ever after.

Somehow, she had gotten a glamorous job and had new friends, if only for six weeks. What would it lead to?

Once she learned her speeches, her position as a hostess was exhilarating. She was greeting visitors from all over the world and reciting the welcome address about her home state.

"At first, I was nervous," she told her mother on the phone. "The city is huge and the streets and subways are filled with people rushing in every direction. The buildings are so tall, much more than downtown Chicago."

"The crowds at the Fair are so pushy and loud. No one follows directions," Abbie said. "But when I get up to the microphone, I feel a rush of excitement."

The weather that summer of 1965 was stifling, making the hot, humid nights uncomfortable in the apartment where the six girls stayed. Abbie shared a tiny bedroom, with lumpy twin beds, with Allison, an exquisite blonde, blue-eyed beauty from Southern Illinois.

"My roommate looks like Miss America," Abbie told Roz. "We talk about Allison's boyfriend, a gorgeous cadet at West Point."

The military academy was north of the city and on her days off, Allison was on a train to visit her guy.

When Abbie could sleep in the suffocating surroundings, she dreamed of meeting a man like Johnny and living happily ever after.

One evening, Abbie was greeting people in the courtyard of the pavilion. The sun had started to set, when two young men approached her. They looked like they were in college.

One fellow was medium height, a little pudgy, with curly dark hair and plastic rimmed sunglasses. He had on a short-sleeved denim shirt and slightly baggy chino pants. Their eyes met and they looked at each other.

He looks like a nice, regular guy, probably smart, thought Abbie. *Not my type, though.*

His buddy was tall and slim with a striped sport shirt and well-fitting blue jeans. His hair had a reddish hue and his eyes were deep cocoa brown. He gave Abbie a friendly smile.

He said to his buddy, "Mel, do you want to see this show?"

Drained from a long day of talking, Abbie hardly noticed what they were saying.

"What's special about the Illinois show?" he asked. "How long is the presentation?"

"It's one of the best shows here," she said. "Have you heard about audio-animatronics? Lincoln actually speaks."

"If we don't like it, can we walk out?" he said staring at her.

"Anyone who would want to walk out doesn't deserve to see it in the first place," Abbie said.

"IIa!" he said, smirking. The two fellows glanced at each other and walked away towards the next pavilion.

"Wait a minute. Please. My name is Abbie and I'm telling you. You will love the show. It's really amazing."

"For that smile we'll come back," the redhead said with a wink.

Abbie stared at him, stuck on his face. "My shift is almost over."

"Good to know. I'm Jeff Enders and this is Mel," he said. "We're home from law school and don't want to miss the fair."

"Come, let me take you in," Abbie said. "Follow me past these exhibits of my home state."

"You'll get to see the last show."

About 30 minutes later, the men came out of the theater and looked for Abbie.

"We loved the show. Old Abe Lincoln did a great job," Jeff said.

She laughed as she was signing out for the day.

"I'm exhausted," she said. "But there's a party at the North Carolina pavilion. Want to come with me?"

They fell into step walking leisurely towards the adjacent area. She couldn't ignore the butterflies in her stomach.

At the party, hundreds of people mingled, bumping into each other. "Hey, don't you work over at Illinois?" one guy asked her.

"Let's get out of here," said Jeff, grabbing Abbie's hand. "Are you available this evening?"

"No plans, I was just going to collapse in my apartment."

They went to drop off his friend Mel in the parking lot. He gently pulled Abbie into a hug. "Can we go back to your place?" The heat was stifling and there was no air conditioning in the apartment, but she agreed.

"You know, I have five roommates, but if you don't mind."

Abbie confiding in her diary, wrote: *"You could hardly breathe the air was so thick. It was unbearably muggy and motionless, like being in a hot bubble. Jeff and I were two sticky bodies clasped together. He felt like Adonis in my arms. Oh! I wanted it to last forever."*

She couldn't get enough of Jeff's lips and his lean body pressed to hers. "I've never had sex with anyone," she told him. "This is not going to be the night."

The law student was disappointed but respected her wishes.

Jeff told her about his life.

"I grew up in Staten Island. I'm in my second year of law school in Baltimore. I like you and want to see you again. Not sure when or where. This week I might be moving from my apartment and will have a new phone number. Will you call me collect in Baltimore?"

If they missed each other, he promised to reach her at the pavilion.

"I won't see you for a week," he kept repeating and pressed her closer. "I know we just met, but you make me crazy."

He took a strand of her damp hair and tucked it behind her ear. Finally, the oppressive heat made her force him to leave.

"I can't wait to hear from you on Wednesday," Jeff said going out the door, all the while staring at her. "Remember, call collect."

The next day and the next, Abbie counted the hours until Wednesday. When the day came, Abbie dialed an operator and placed the collect call. The phone kept ringing and ringing. The operator said, "I'm sorry, the party does not answer. Would you like to try again?"

During her break, Abbie tried again. She called the next day, but no Jeff. The information operator told her there was no listing for a Jeff Enders, but a listing for a Brian Enders, and the number was the one she had. She figured it must be his father's name, but it still did not make sense.

The following Saturday night, Abbie got a call from Jeff's friend, Mel. "Hi, remember me? Jeff and I met you last week."

"Sure, how's your friend?"

"I don't really know. We aren't that friendly," said Mel. "We just happened to run into each other that night."

"Do you know if Jeff moved? He said he was changing apartments."

"I don't think he moved. You never know with him. Want to go out with me?"

"No, Mel. Sorry. I'm getting ready to go back to Chicago."

It was a turning point for Abbie. The beginning of her love affair — not with Jeff — but with New York City.

"Will I ever meet anyone?" she wrote in her diary. *"Where will I end up?"*

Many years later, Abbie still remembered her singular night with Jeff, the handsome law student. The heat of the night, the chemistry they had…it was a permanent memory sketched in her impressionable brain. Years later, she looked him up on the internet. He became the CEO and founder of a fast food restaurant chain and had been married to a famous actress for 10 years. The article stated that they were divorced.

Chapter Six

Toward the end of her stint at the World's Fair, Abbie invited her friend Roz to fly up from Chicago for the weekend.

"It's my last week. Why don't you come out? There's an empty bed in our apartment. It's grungy, but you can stay for a few days," Abbie said. "We'll go into Manhattan. There are lots of cool places to hang out."

On Friday night, Abbie and Roz were set to go to a new hangout called Friday's and invited Jan.

"I would love to go," Jan said. "I know my way around the Upper East Side. We take the IRT train to East 59th Street and Lexington."

When they got off the subway, the girls climbed up the stairs and walked north, then east to First Avenue looking for Friday's restaurant, the new place everyone was raving about.

A newspaper article said the name was a shortened version of Thank God It's Friday (TGIF), a hip new singles saloon serving cheeseburgers, onion rings, chicken wings, and casual fare on red-and-white checkered tablecloths. Big bowls of peanuts in the shell were strategically placed. Shells were all over the floor amidst sawdust.

The restaurant reeked of beer and cigarette smoke. Finding a spot at the dramatic mahogany bar, Abbie said, "We don't have to stay long. Let's have a drink and a bite to eat."

In a week, they would all be back in Illinois. "I am going to miss this city," Abbie said. She was going back to a substitute teaching job in Chicago.

"Daddy is waiting for me to work at his office." Jan groaned, taking a swig of her cold, frosty beer.

Roz said, "Back to the insurance business grind. And Bob, my true love, who won't make a commitment."

"What's the story with that?" Abbie said. "He's too good-looking to be a husband."

"I think he's looking for a rich girl," Roz said. "I'm just a cute blonde without a college degree."

Suddenly, out of the buzzing, hazy room, a tall, strapping man with twinkling blue eyes approached Abbie, closing in on her like a bullet. She took a step forward into the crowd, toward him.

"Hi. Gee, it's crowded. Not easy pushing my way to you," he said with a big grin showing straight white teeth. "I was thinking, I've got to meet that girl over there."

"My name is Marty Rifkin, hometown is Jersey City, but live uptown on First. What about you?"

"Well, hi." She took a puff of the cigarette she was pretending to smoke.

"I'm Abbie Seligman, say hello to my friends, Jan and Roz."

"Hi ladies. It's a pleasure." His eyes didn't move from Abbie's face. "Is this your first time here?"

"Oh, well, yes. We've been working at the World's Fair for the summer and Roz came for a visit."

"That's fantastic. Wow," he said. "What's your job?"

They talked a long time trying to talk and hear above the noise. "What do you do?" she asked him.

"I'm an engineer, right now doing projects for NASA. You know, they are planning a trip to the moon."

Marty was 25 years old and liked to laugh, in between chats. He wrote Abbie's phone number on a napkin and promised to come to the fair the next night when she got off her shift.

Later that night, Abbie wrote in her diary: *Too bad I'm meeting this great guy a week before leaving.*

True to his word, Marty showed up the next evening at the fair. When Abbie got off her shift at about 5 pm, he was waiting in the courtyard. When she saw him, her heart started to beat like a drum. He hugged her. She had to look up at him. He was over six feet tall, with smooth light brown hair and when he talked, his blue eyes squinted. He laughed a lot and had opinions about everything, even Lincoln's Gettysburg Address.

In her diary, Abbie wrote: *"Marty has a perpetual smile on his face. He told me to enjoy life, be cheerful. Extend yourself beyond yourself."*

He has so many requirements, she thought.

His favorite line was: "It's copacetic."

Abbie had to look it up in a dictionary.

She decided she was not at all copacetic, at least, not according to the definition. She was the consummate self-conscious introvert, searching desperately for a comfortable path to follow.

On that first date, Marty was already lecturing her about love, saying it was a rational knowledge. "Joy is the simple pleasures of the moment. Unhappy people are the losers, but they have so much to be happy about," he said in his diatribes as they walked around the city.

Abbie admired this outgoing guy's opinions and mannerisms, noting in her diary: *"I'm trying to be more cheerful. Through my new teacher, I'm learning that I must consciously extend myself to others if I'm going to find satisfaction in my life."*

After knowing Marty for one day, he had gotten to her. Abbie pondered his philosophy, thinking he was right. *Maybe I could change myself from a scared, over-analytical, shy girl to a lively, joyful person.*

She practically had to skip to keep up with Marty on their first date. In his 1963 white Chevrolet, they went to his neighborhood on the Upper East Side of the city. He found a parking spot on 85th Street.

They walked over to his studio apartment on Second Avenue, a tiny walk-up over a small grocery store. There was one flight of stairs leading to the second and third floors. The lighting fixture was a single bulb, the walls were white brick.

"It's my first apartment since college," he said.

"Where did you go?" Abbie wanted to know.

"Upsala College in New Jersey. I played baseball there. On a scholarship."

At dinner in a casual steak place, he told her about his family. He had six brothers and a sister. His parents were from a village in Austria and had come to the States before the war started. Now they had a big, old house in Jersey City.

Abbie was fascinated by his large family. "Are you all close?"

"Yes, we actually are. I'm especially tight with a couple of my brothers and my sister, who is a sweetheart."

She wanted to remember every detail of that day, every nuance of his speech, especially his Jersey accent, the blond hairs on his muscular arms, the touch of his lips the first time they kissed. With every moment, she melted, falling into a spell.

After dinner, they walked slowly back to his studio and fell onto his lumpy bed. He folded her in his arms and kissed her gently for a long time. She couldn't remember when they undressed. It was all a dreamy haze.

They made love the whole night. She willingly gave up her virginity, so naturally that it was like breathing. That night, she became a joyful woman.

Early in the morning, they were limp from emotion and they both called in to their jobs to say they were sick. They drank coffee and devoured buttered toast, showered, then leisurely walked to the Metropolitan Museum of Art on Fifth Avenue. Abbie was struck by the mid-century architecture of the townhomes and brownstones on the Upper East Side streets.

"Wouldn't it be wonderful to live in one of these houses?" she said.

"Maybe, but I'm more of a suburban guy," Marty said.

On that perfect, sun-filled New York day in late August of 1965, fluffy white clouds dangled in the clear blue sky. Abbie and Marty walked hand in hand, sometimes their arms slipped easily around each other.

"I feel like I have known you my whole life," Marty said.

The lovers roamed the museum for hours and at lunch they devoured hot dogs on the front steps. In Marty's apartment later that day, Abbie realized she wanted to stay in New York. It wasn't just about Marty. The city made her feel alive like she never had before. She had already figured out the grid system: north, south, east, and west, uptown and downtown. People moving in every direction, the buses and subway trains, and the multitude of restaurants and diners on every street captivated her.

She remembered about the fellowship at Columbia University. Maybe they had gotten an opening.

Why not call up the school? She felt empowered by new-found love. While Marty went down to the market, Abbie dialed up the college and got through to the special education department, asking for the director. Miraculously, he came to the phone.

"Hello, this is Professor Connor."

"Hello, Dr. Connor. This is Abbie Seligman. I'm calling about the fellowship program. I'm on the wait list and I thought that possibly there might have been a cancellation. Uh, possibly there's an opening."

The professor barely paused. "Yes, I recall your name on our list. You're the student from Chicago. As a matter of fact, we just had a cancellation. We would have to review your file with the committee and get back to you before school starts."

"Well, I am so glad I reached you. Thank you very much," she said. "I hope to hear from you soon."

Marty returned carrying a big bag of groceries.

"Marty, you will not believe what just happened. I called Columbia and they might have an opening for me," she said. She was practically floating.

He put down the groceries and took her in his arms. "That is a lucky try. You may end up living in New York."

The professor had assured her they would let her know within the week. The program was beginning in two weeks.

On closing day at the fair, there was a farewell party with a mass exchange of phone numbers. "You are all invited as guests to stay in my house in Springfield for Thanksgiving," Janet said.

Abbie said her final goodbye to Marty, believing that somehow, she would see him again. "Call me when you get home," he said.

She secured a ride back to Illinois with a co-worker going home to Aurora. From there, Abbie picked up a train to the north side of Chicago. When she finally arrived, she ran home to find her father waiting for her. She hugged him tightly.

"I have a surprise for you. You got a telegram," he said.

"A telegram! From who?" She had never gotten a telegram in her life.

Her father handed her an envelope with a telegram inside that said Columbia Teachers College.

It read: *Dear Miss Seligman, you have been accepted into the teacher training program for a master's degree in deaf education. Orientation is scheduled to begin on September 4 at the Lexington School for the Deaf on 68th Street and Lexington Avenue.*

She jumped up and down, hugging her dad.

"What should I do? Daddy, I don't know what to do."

Her father, usually quiet without much to say, hugged her. "You should take it, Abbie. Take it." His voice, his firm answer, surprised her. He had made the decision for her. She immediately thought of Marty and what he would think. They had gone through their final good-byes and did not expect to see each other again. Would he be happy about her coming back? Later that night, she hesitated, but called him.

"How are you?" he greeted her warmly. "I'm glad to hear from you." He sounded surprised and genuinely happy about the news.

Later to her parents, Abbie said, "It wouldn't change my mind or my decision, but it would be a lot easier to know the guy was crazy about me and wanted me to come back."

"It's a real honor to be accepted at Columbia," Marty had told her. "You deserve it and I can't wait to see you."

No invitations were made, but she would not have considered staying with him. It was not appropriate for a young woman to live with a young man she hardly knew. *Even if I already slept with him.*

Chapter Seven
Landed in September 1965.

LaGuardia was jammed with travelers. Abbie waited to claim her baggage and then rushed to get a taxi. She felt lost but excited to be back in the vibrant city where she would be moving on with her life.

After accepting the academic fellowship, Abbie called friends to see if anyone knew where she could stay temporarily in New York.

"You could always stay for a few days in a hotel," a friend said. "There's one for women called the Barbizon. It's near Bloomingdale's department store."

"If it doesn't work out, you can always come home," her dad reminded her.

"I'm worried," her mother said, frowning. "You don't know anyone in that crazy city."

Abbie knew she was taking a chance showing up in New York City without a permanent place to stay, but the fellowship was hers. She knew in her heart this was meant to be. Nothing much was holding her in Chicago: a substitute teaching job, a few friends, most of whom were already married.

On the phone with Marty, she felt tempted to ask him for help. She wanted, however, to be an independent woman.

He had said, "I can't wait to see you, but I have to work. Otherwise I'd pick you up at the airport. Let's meet after you settle in at your friend's place."

The friend she had located was a girl she knew from high school. Savvy and sassy Liz Barfield had recently moved to New York and was looking for a job. When Abbie called her from Chicago, Liz offered to share her apartment for a week.

"Truthfully, I need the money," Liz said. "I live in a nice new building on the Upper East Side."

A yellow cab took Abbie from LaGuardia through the enormous borough of Queens. A sea of cars speeded on the expressway toward Manhattan, past a vast cemetery of gravesites, past mid-rise brick apartment buildings, skyscrapers, and over clanking steel bridges.

As they reached the 59th Street bridge, countless people could be noticed dashing for buses. Everyone was in a hurry, rushing, and scurrying to get to work or school on time.

Abbie spotted overflowing garbage cans and congested corners where nervous pedestrians waited for the lights to change. The cacophony of honking cars and cabs and braking buses made Abbie realize that she was a long way from home.

Abbie wiped her sweaty palms on her dress as they neared the Upper East Side of the city. She felt her heart pound. The taxi dropped her at East 72nd Street close to the river. The white brick high-rise building was just a few years old. A doorman came out to the curb and peeked in the window. He opened the car door and helped Abbie out.

"Hi, I'm staying with Liz Barfield in Apt. 12J," said Abbie. He handily removed her two suitcases out of the trunk of the Yellow Cab and guided her to the elevator.

Going up to Liz's apartment was strange. She knew her from passing in the hallways of her high school and from the neighborhood where they lived. In between classes, they used to hang out at the same grungy luncheonette across from school.

If I didn't need a place to stay so badly, I would never have contacted her. She always acted uppity, so sure of herself. Well, I'm here now.

In that moment before the door opened, Abbie made a quick vow to make the best of it. Liz answered the door in jeans and a gray t-shirt, looking thinner than she remembered. She had pretty blue eyes and a short pageboy haircut.

"Hi, come on in," Liz said with a deadpan look. "I'm glad you are here but let's be honest. You need a place to stay for a few days, and I can hardly pay the rent. So, the money will come in handy.

"I've got a new roommate coming in two weeks. My job situation isn't terrific. I'm trying to get something in marketing, but all they want to know is how fast I can type."

"It's okay. I just need a place until I find something. It won't take me long." She glanced around. "It's a nice apartment."

The large windows had spotless white venetian blinds. There was a dark blue couch and a small wooden dining table with two chairs. One lounge chair was near the window and a big throw pillow was on the floor. The kitchen was brand new, painted white, as was everything in the apartment. It looked sterile, except for a toaster oven and a coffee pot, a four-burner gas stove, and a standard-size Frigidaire. Liz was neat as a pin. You could give her credit for that.

Liz answered, "It's a safe doorman building and I'm lucky to have gotten a lease, since I have no job yet. My father had to co-sign."

Liz showed Abbie where she would sleep in the alcove off the living room and reminded her that she had to take out the garbage once a day. "I'm not anyone's maid."

Abbie was struck by her blunt talk. She felt awkward in someone else's apartment, but it would just be for a few days.

She was bound to meet someone at school who would be her roommate. She had a $2,000 stipend from Columbia and if worse came to worse, she would have to stay in a women's hotel for a while.

On her first full day, before graduate school started, Abbie took the bus uptown to meet Marty at the Copper Kettle coffee shop on First Avenue and 84th Street near his studio. It was an old-fashioned diner with red plastic booths and green Formica counters with swivel seats.

Marty gave her a tender kiss, wrapping her in his strong arms. He looked as handsome as she remembered him. They sat down at a booth and ordered coffee. The waitress, dressed in a red cotton pinafore type dress, promptly brought over two oversized white mugs with a steamy brew. She handed them each a menu.

"I can't believe you are here, that you came back," said Marty. "How is your living arrangement?"

"A disaster. I hardly know Liz. She's a mean girl from my high school. Once I meet my classmates, I hope to find an apartment with someone."

"If you have any trouble, I'll help you work something out."

They ordered bacon and eggs and had their coffee refilled. Abbie looked around at the clientele, mostly young women in shorts or cut-off jeans. It was still blazing hot outside. Some girls had on cotton sundresses in pastel colors; they all had on sandals with polish on their toenails. Most of the men were under the age of 30, clean cut and wearing chinos or jeans.

"I'll tell you what, let's take a day tour of downtown Manhattan," said Marty. "Do you feel like it?"

"Yes," Abbie said, drowning in his blue eyes. She was more infatuated with him than ever.

Marty got out tokens and led her to the subway entrance and through a turnstile where a big sign read IRT downtown. They took the train to the South Street Seaport and strolled around.

"This is one of my favorite parts of the city," Marty said. "You know, I grew up in Jersey City near the water and played a lot of ball. That was my favorite thing to do. I played more at college."

Marty gently squeezed her hand and they walked slowly past cozy cafes and casual restaurants. Abbie immediately loved the funky mix of boutiques and mom-and-pop shops. She noticed the classic old buildings on Water Street and Fulton Street. Some looked like they were built during the Revolutionary War.

"It's so different here," she said. "Do you love it? There's so much charm and excitement."

"New York is a city of diversity. Some people like it, some don't. Over there," he said, pointing to a huge vacant lot where construction equipment was set up next to a deep hole in the ground, they're building a skyscraper. It will have businesses and a shopping center with more than 100 floors of offices. They're calling it the World Trade Center."

Marty showed her around Wall Street and part of the financial district where they passed a tall church with an old graveyard.

"We're on Broadway and this is Trinity Church. The cemetery is a historic landmark where hundreds of old souls are buried."

"It looks like it's been here a long time," Abbie said.

"I read that members of the first Continental Congress are buried here. For one, Alexander Hamilton." He glanced at his watch.

"We'll have to do more of this another time. I'm going to have to get back."

He hailed a passing yellow taxi and they got in.

In the cab, he said, "Honey, what are your plans for the rest of the day?"

"I have some shopping to do to get ready for school."

"Sorry to be in a hurry. I've got to do some work."

When they reached the building where she was staying, Marty kissed her lightly good-bye.

"Let's talk later and get together for dinner," he said.

Abbie felt unsettled over the abrupt departure. She understood, though, that Marty was interested in helping her get grounded. But he had things to do.

I'm not sure where this is going, she thought. *But I'm in love.*

Chapter Eight

When she entered the Lexington School for the Deaf on Orientation Day, Abbie was relieved to see a small crowd of young women, much like herself, and a few young men, talking comfortably to each other. They were all picking up name tags from a big table and greeting the school staff.

Vaulted ceilings and marble floors made the lobby look grander and larger than it was. It was a school that dated back to 1939. Wooden panels exhibited pictures of the school's early history, showing the prominent founders and board members and photos of teachers and children in classrooms. Auditory training equipment, desks, and chalkboards were educational décor.

Despite the heat, Abbie felt comfortable in the clothes she had decided to wear. Rather than a dress or pants, Abbie had chosen a loose skirt and short-sleeved blouse under a light linen blazer. At the last minute, she had put on thin gold hoops and a tiny pearl necklace. She tried to ignore the lingering September heat, but her auburn hair curled in the humidity. Beads of dampness clung to the back of her neck and underarms.

Abbie quickly blended with the small crowd and soon found herself talking to a plain-looking girl with soft straight brown hair and a dusting of freckles on her nose and cheeks. Glancing at Abbie's name tag, the girl spoke in a friendly tone.

"Hi, Abbie, my name is Claire Adelson. Where are you from?"

Her voice was gentle and sweet with an obvious Southern accent.

"I'm from Chicago. What about you?"

"Lexington, Kentucky. My boyfriend came here with me and he's staying with a friend from Las Vegas."

"Nice. What does your boyfriend do?"

"Joe is in advertising and he just started with an agency here," Claire said. "His father is in the casino business in Las Vegas."

"That's great," Abbie said. "Do you have an apartment yet? I'm staying with a friend for a week while I hunt a place. Do you know of any?"

"There's a new building a block from here on Third Avenue and they're renting. Would you go there with me and have a look?"

"I would love to."

Claire seems like such a nice girl. She was sweet and totally a Southern belle type. Abbie took to her immediately.

During their lunch break, the two girls went to the rental office and signed a lease for a studio for $168 a month. It was an ordinary square room with a dressing alcove and an adequate kitchen with a window. From the back window they could see the Russian Embassy on the side street.

On the phone later, Abbie told her mother she had found a roommate.

"We signed on for a year in this apartment right near school," Abbie said. "It's in a new building."

Her mother asked, "Do you have enough money?"

"I have about $500 in my checking account. The college is sending part of my stipend in a week. I think I can get by for now. Claire's mother is already sending us linens and bedspreads. Her boyfriend found end tables to put next to our beds."

Soon, the teacher trainees were immersed in educational routines, followed by classes at Columbia University in the late afternoon and early evenings. Abbie and most of her classmates didn't get home until about nine at night.

Abbie spent weekends with Marty. They hung out in his shabby little apartment and made love on and off all day long on an extra-long single bed. On Sundays, they went out to dinner at a neighborhood steak joint, called Beggi's. It was always crowded and noisy with young people drinking beer and eating hamburgers and grilled rib steaks served with heaps of French fries.

Every Sunday night after Marty dropped her off, Abbie called her mother and sometimes her best friend Roz to let them know what was going on in her new life. She tried not to brag because she wasn't all that confident.

"School is hard work, but I'm learning so much," said Abbie. "It's all an exciting adventure, but the biggest thrill is Marty. I have never felt like this about any other guy."

She left out the part about all the dirty dishes in his tiny kitchen sink. *I don't have to wash them, but how can I just leave them there?*

She also left out the part about his incessant lecturing about living in the moment, about the copacetic lifestyle, and free love.

Abbie wrote one night in her diary: *I think he's the one. He's my future husband.* Another night she was less confident, writing: *I am starting to feel nervous and scared of losing him. I overanalyze everything he says to me.*

As their relationship grew and became routine, she became fixated on her lover, depending on him for all her time away from school and student teaching. His diatribes about living in the moment, savoring the joys of life, set the spontaneity standard for how she should feel. She judged herself by his reactions to things she said, particularly trivial remarks she made offhandedly like a simple schoolgirl.

If she mentioned that her hair was messed up, or that she had a headache and was tired, he would send her a disapproving glance.

"You're always thinking about superficial stuff," Marty would say. "You need to grow up and be a woman."

At those times, Abbie would shrivel up inside and dwell on his disapproval, letting it eat away at her self-esteem. Other times, she was too absorbed by the students and teachers and hardly gave his negative comments a thought.

Abbie had found a home in a famous city in the center of the universe. *I'm going to make it here. One way or another.*

Chapter Nine

In 1965, the teacher training program at the Lexington School for the Deaf was centered around oral speech and natural language for hearing impaired children. Teachers trained in this method were experienced in presenting lessons based on real-life situations that elicited speech and natural language. American Sign Language (ASL) was prohibited.

Bea Hart, a veteran in the educational field, was the head of the training program. She spoke passionately about oral education for hearing impaired children, including the profoundly deaf. Hart advocated for the development of language skills, spoken and written, and emphasized auditory training and lip reading.

Every day the trainees observed lessons prepared for young hearing-impaired children, all of whom wore dual hearing aids to maximize their residual hearing. Though many of the students were profoundly deaf, amplification provided auditory cues while lip reading provided visual cues.

Memorable lessons were designed to elicit language. For example, idioms such as "he's in hot water" or "it cost an arm and a leg" were staged to prompt responses. If it was raining hard, the teacher would ask "How hard is it raining"?

The children might answer, "It's raining a lot. It's raining so much." With their hands, they might mimic the rain.

"It's raining cats and dogs," Mrs. Gang said. She taught the children to orally repeat and write sentences.

Another lesson might be staged to demonstrate adjectives, such as beautiful, scary, hard, soft, mushy, or moist. Using real objects, pictures and context, an animated teacher would elicit words and phrases from the young children. Speech correction would take place as needed. The words and phrases would be coaxed into sentence format, verbal and written.

"That's right," said the teacher. "The bread is soft. Is the chalk board soft? Is the desk hard? No, the board is hard, the desk is hard."

Questions were posed to the children. "Do you want the red ball or the blue ball?" "Give me a full sentence." A child might answer, "I want the blue ball."

Each morning, the teacher would write on oversized newsprint sheets placed on a stand. With a magic marker, she would ask, "What day is today?" "Is it sunny"? The responses would be recorded and repeated aloud.

The program at the Lexington School for the Deaf had evolved over the years to become the number one school on the East Coast dedicated to oral language and speech.

Periodically, the teachers in training were taken on trips to visit other schools: Northampton School for the Deaf in Massachusetts, Gallaudet College in Washington, DC, and the New York School for the Deaf where natural language and ASL were combined in the curriculum. At

Gallaudet College, ASL was the primary form of communication.

When not completely absorbed by training and academic classes at night, Abbie worried.

What will happen when the school year is over? Will I be able to get a teaching job in New York? I'll have to support myself or get married — or go home.

Abbie's roommate Claire was eager to go back home and get married. She and her fiancé had a wedding planned in Lexington, Kentucky, her hometown.

"Joe says we'll live in Las Vegas and work for his father at a casino. He's not really doing well in New York."

One night, Abbie asked Claire, "What do I do about Marty? Is he serious?"

"He's always with you. Come straight out and ask him about your future. Is he thinking about marriage and a family?"

Abbie wrote in her diary: *I found the courage to leave Chicago, to escape from my dominating mother, and quiet as a mouse father, but I'm afraid to question Marty, to honestly voice my feelings.*

Affection came naturally between them, but there was no mention of commitment. No talk of a future together.

Marty's family considered them to be a serious couple.

"I'm afraid to ask him if we're going to get married," she told Roz. "I don't want to scare him away with any kind of ultimatum."

"I'm not the right person to advise you. I just broke up with Bob," Roz said. "He met someone else."

In the 1960s, women waited for the man to make the move. Passive behavior rather than assertive action was

Abbie's *modus operandi*. At night, she tossed and turned in bed while her roommate Claire slept peacefully across the room in their cozy studio. She knew her fiancé adored her and the big diamond ring on her finger shone bright.

In 1965, Abbie feared rejection and abandonment. She could only write in her diary: *Marty will turn out the same as the other guys I liked back home, those who didn't choose me.*

She was only 21 years old, but all her friends back home in Chicago were married or about to get married to their high school or college sweethearts.

"Is this your first meaningful relationship?" her classmate Debbie asked.

"I guess so. I've had summer romances, prom dates, blind dates," she said. "But I stayed a virgin, until Marty."

Abbie thought about their weekends. Walking around the Upper East Side, the Village, and riding bikes in Central Park. On Marty's turf, Abbie took her first tumble into the waves at the Jersey shore. Often, they went to family parties and picnics where the brothers played catch with their sons and nephews.

At the end of each dreamy weekend, Abbie dreaded saying good night. She clung to Marty's big frame at the door of her apartment, her arms wrapped around him. Parting was usually met not with reassurance, but lectures about the copacetic philosophy.

"You have to relax, enjoy each moment," Marty said.

Finally, nine months into the relationship, they lay entwined on the narrow lumpy bed in his studio.

"What will happen is that one day we will just go and get married," he said.

Stunned, Abbie lay motionless. "Do you mean it? Do you think we will get married?"

She took a huge breath of relief, and a sweet calm washed over her. For many months, she held on to those words, kept them as her litany whenever panic set in.

One day, we will just go and get married, we will get married, get married.

Chapter Ten

Spring came. Then early summer. The teacher training program was coming to an end. Everyone in the class was graduating and everyone was scrambling to find jobs. Some planned to go on for more training in audiology and speech pathology.

Most of the new teachers were headed back to their home states, but she and her friend Debbie wanted to stay in New York, where there were only a few schools that focused on oral/aural education for the deaf.

"My studio lease is up. My roommate is going home. I have to find a place to live," Abbie told Debbie.

"I know, my apartment lease is ended too. There are some girls I know who we might be able to live with, at least for the summer."

Many young women in the city were in change mode, searching for relationships and careers. She and Debbie temporarily moved in with two other women in a sublet apartment on East 69th Street.

Susan Lerner, a cute brunette, had a perpetual grin on her face and was usually giggling as she got ready to run across the street to her boyfriend's apartment. She would take a shower, slip on a raincoat, and dash across First Avenue. If her parents called from North Carolina, the girls would say she was out for dinner.

Sheila Stern, a tiny dark-haired paralegal from Atlanta, was turning 30 and was desperate to find a guy. She was fixed up with a handsome stockbroker about two inches taller than she was. They seemed a perfect couple and Sheila prayed it would become serious.

"If this doesn't work out, I'm going back home."

One evening Marty said, "I have some bad news. My job is being phased out."

"You never mentioned any problems. What are you going to do?"

"I have to start looking for a new job and it's a bad time for engineers."

By early September, the summer roommates were splitting up, going on with other arrangements. In a panic, Abbie finally confronted Marty about living arrangements, and he said somberly, "I'm just not ready to make a commitment."

"I love you, but I don't have a job," he said. "I know I've disappointed you, but the time is not right."

As Abbie prepared to move out of her summer sublet, she checked the calendar and gasped. *Oh my God, my period is late.* Two weeks late. She hadn't been using birth control.

"I am an idiot," she said to Debbie. On the phone, she told Marty she could possibly be pregnant. He stammered, "Well, sweetheart, how did that happen?"

Well, my guess is when you have sex seven times on Sundays, it's possible to get pregnant. We never talked about using birth control. You never brought it up."

There was silence. The good news was that she hadn't been with anyone else.

"Well, if I do have a baby, at least I will know who the father is," she said.

Abortions were illegal in the United States. Her friend in Chicago was forced to go to Puerto Rico and another friend flew to Switzerland.

The next couple of weeks passed in a blur. In Abbie's nightmares, she heard a baby crying. Her mother was screaming at her and her father was shaking his head.

In the midst of her pregnancy panic, she and Debbie were offered teaching jobs at a school for the deaf in the Bronx.

A friend advised Abbie to take a very hot bath. "Make it very hot," she said.

To her relief, Abbie's period showed up.

Abbie knew the exciting romance with Marty was waning. She couldn't count on him, and she wasn't sure any more he was the guy for her. She had thought he was her true love, but he couldn't make a commitment. He wasn't ready.

Why? I wish I knew.

Chapter Eleven

St. Joseph's School for the Deaf in the Bronx, about 20 miles north of Manhattan, was run by an order of nuns who dressed in plain clothes instead of religious habits. Their usual attire was buttoned up light wool dresses and laced-up shoes. Their mission was to educate hearing impaired children and prepare them for productive lives.

The three-story building was constructed of beautiful red brick situated off a major highway called the Hutchinson River Parkway near the neighborhood of Eastchester. Previously, the school had been located in Brooklyn and relocated to the Bronx in 1913 to serve the growing population of deaf children.

Whenever practicable for the student, the religious order believed in the oral approach to education of hearing-impaired children, teaching speech and lip reading. For other students that needed to communicate in signs, the school incorporated American Sign Language.

Sister Mary Elizabeth hired Abbie at the first interview and assigned her to a fifth-grade class of five students who were considered to have high potential for verbal and written communication. Debbie got a similar teaching position at the second-grade level.

Elated, Debbie and Abbie teamed up to find an apartment in their neighborhood on the Upper East Side, near their summer sublet. They discovered that the best way to find a rental was to walk around and talk to the doormen; they knew everything about which tenants were moving out. For a $5 tip, apartment hunters, especially young women, could find out about an available apartment and be ready with a deposit to the landlord.

Within days, the friends found a two-bedroom apartment on East 70th Street between Second and Third Avenues in a white-brick, elevator and doorman building, and immediately signed a one-year lease.

"I'm so excited," Abbie said. "We are New Yorkers with real jobs and an apartment."

"We've got one year to find husbands," Debbie said, pointing her finger at Abbie. "Otherwise, I have to go home to Buffalo." The clock was ticking.

Abbie laughed, but it wasn't funny. "By age 25, we will be considered undesirable old maids."

They calculated the amount of money they would need for a year's rent and quickly realized they needed two additional roommates. They placed an ad in *The New York Times* "Roommates Wanted" column. They borrowed shopping carts from the supermarket to move their belongings from their summer sublets on 69th Street to their new apartment a block away.

After unpacking, they went out to celebrate at Friday's. They made plans at a front row table covered with a red-and-white checkered table cloth, chomping on hamburgers and French fries, contemplating the year ahead. They decided to splurge on a decanter of red house wine. Abbie looked about for Marty, but there was no sign of him. Soon a couple of young men stopped to talk and flirt; the girls were invited to a singles party the next night. The boys were both from Brooklyn and had just gotten jobs downtown at Dean Witter, an investment firm.

Abbie loved their new place, within walking distance to restaurants and singles bars and near the Lexington Avenue subway line. She kept thinking how spacious it was with two bedrooms and two bathrooms, a big living room and a dining area. She and Debbie took a bus to the nearest Salvation Army outlet where they picked up a few pieces of furniture, including used twin beds and bedroom dressers for only $5 each.

The superintendent gifted them with a sofa and living-room chairs that had seen life in a vacated apartment.

"Thank you, Carlos," Abbie said. "Is there any way to turn down the heat…it's so hot here."

"Sorry, you'll have to keep the windows open."

"I guess this is what we have to put up with to live in New York," Abbie said to Debbie, who was putting away her clothes in the old wood dresser.

Over the weekend, they started to get phone calls from the ad they had placed for roommates. Several women came to meet them and see the apartment. They were all young and doing office work.

Two of the women were opposites in personality and temperament. Yvonne, a French-speaking girl from the Isle of Rhodes, was serious, dark-haired, petite, with big brown eyes like the Keane paintings and thin pressed lips. Both Abbie and Debbie liked her somber demeanor, thinking ahead that she would be reliable and pay her share of the rent on time. Her French-speaking cousins lived on the Upper West Side and they looked after her.

"I'm working for a foreign bank, in the currency trading department," Yvonne said. "My fluency in French got me the position."

Debbie and Abbie looked at each other and raised their eyebrows. "Wow, that's neat," Abbie said.

In those days, it was unusual for a woman to be working in a bank. The other women they knew or met all taught school or worked in an office.

Yvonne made Turkish coffee every morning. She stirred the thick brew repeatedly as she pursed her thin lips. Then, she would trudge off to midtown in her dark business jacket and skirt with high heels. As soon as she came home in the evening, she tossed off her shoes.

Yvonne always groaned about her job. "Oh, what a day. My boss wants me to trade bonds and I have to study for a license."

The roommates were on tight budgets so they usually cooked every night except when they had dates. Yvonne was the main cook in the house. She regularly sautéed white rice in butter, added water, salt and pepper, brought it to a boil, then simmered it as a side dish for their meat or chicken entree. She delicately applied Dijon mustard to the skin of the chicken and placed it under the broiler until it was brown and crispy.

Phyllis, the fourth roommate, a vivacious girl from Connecticut, had a muscular frame and walked with an athletic gait. She constantly smoked cigarettes. Abbie didn't mind because she liked to occasionally mooch. Phyllis knew all the best hangouts on the Upper East Side and went out almost every night.

On a long-distance phone call to Roz in Chicago, Abbie said, "I can't stop thinking about Marty, but we are having a wonderful time here. There are so many guys to meet, lawyers, doctors, artists, journalists…they are everywhere."

Abbie wrote in her diary: *It's November 1966. Here I am living in New York, the center of the universe, sharing an apartment with three nice women. I have a job teaching in a school for the deaf run by an order of nuns. I found the courage to end a going-nowhere relationship with the boyfriend I've been in love with for more than a year. He's wonderful, but he can't make a commitment.*

As the year went by, Abbie decided to take another step forward. After her breakup with Marty, she realized there *were* other options out there…lots of good catches who were looking for serious relationships. She still had trouble thinking of herself as a woman, but she was beginning to grow up. She made the rounds of parties and bars, met men here and there. Some seemed to be husband material, including one brilliant medical illustrator who sketched pictures of Abbie.

Life in the apartment revolved around the single landline telephone in the front hall. All four women impatiently waited for it to ring to see if dates for Saturday night would materialize. Debbie had been fixed up with a talented, rising, young lawyer and for six months, they went out every Saturday night. She was completely smitten with him. If he didn't call by Wednesday night, she would become depressed. One night she ran so fast for the phone, she fell and broke her elbow.

It was lively Phyllis who was leading the way into adventure. She was circulating around the bars until one Friday night, she went out and did not come home. The roommates did not hear from her for three days. On Monday, she showed up in a jittery state, looking exhausted with hives all over her body. She shakily announced that she had met a guy and they were getting engaged.

As a final fling, Phyllis agreed to go with Abbie on a trip to Europe for three weeks in the summer. They had even bought Eurailpasses and a travel guidebook about decent pensions, where they could stay.

Despite the busy social scene, Abbie hadn't found a spark with any new guy she met. One day in April, just after Debbie and Abbie got home from teaching, the phone rang. Debbie answered, and she looked at Abbie and mouthed, "It's Marty."

Abbie's mouth dropped open in surprise and almost fell backward. Walking toward the phone, she lifted her hands in a thankful gesture to the love goddess she imagined in the sky.

She gripped the phone to her ear and walked in small circles. At first, she and Marty made awkward small talk until he said that he wanted to see her again. "It's been six months since we've seen each other. I miss you."

"I thought it was over. What makes you think you want to see me? I thought I was having a baby and you didn't care."

"Honestly, sweetheart, I think of you every day. When I'm out with other girls, all I can think of is you. I was out with a ballerina and your face kept popping into my head. And I have a new job."

"A ballerina? If that's what you want, go for it," Abbie said.

The news about the job was the best part. *Maybe things could work out.* Abbie thought it was destiny calling. *We are meant for each other. This is going to work out after all.*

All the progress she had made with new friends and connections, gaining confidence and maturity, were thrown to the wind without rational thought. She heard his voice and couldn't wait to see him.

She felt powerless to resist his plea. The familiar cadence of his voice melted away her sense of resistance and again they fell into their old routine. Except, this time, she thought, "*He is so overbearing and opinionated. I hate the way he talks about copacetic crap.*"

And she realized, after some fresh experiences, that he was missing some essential lovemaking techniques. It was all about him always and though she adored the way he looked and walked, threw a softball, his crinkly blue eyes, now she wanted more. She had gained insight. She had read books about lovemaking and wanted something the authors called "foreplay."

One night, a lawyer that Abbie had met at a singles party phoned to let her know that he was putting together a singles house in the Hamptons on Long Island. "Would you like to take a half share in a beautiful new beach house in Amagansett?"

She explained about her boyfriend situation and he said something that struck her. Woke her up to reality.

"I'm not telling you what to do, but you shouldn't put all your eggs in one basket. The share is every other weekend for $150. What do you have to lose?"

She thought about it for just about five seconds. She had heard about the Hamptons, the popular singles scene at the beach way out on Long Island. At the fabulous price quoted, she readily agreed. That same week, a girl named Ellen Pearlman got in touch with her. She was going to be one of the housemates and they decided to meet for dinner. Ellen was from Brooklyn and had been around the singles scene for a long time, searching for Mr. Right.

One night, Ellen called Abbie and they chatted.

"I'd like to meet you for a drink," Ellen said. "We can share notes on finding men in the city. I've been at it for too long."

The two would-be housemates met at a bar on Third Avenue and they dissected single life, the ups and downs. Ellen, a tall woman with bleached blonde hair, appeared soft-spoken, although not what Abbie considered her type. She had dropped out of college and was working as a secretary in a midtown law firm. She talked a lot about a friend of hers who was coming out as a guest in their house.

"I'm in love with this guy named Sam. But he only likes me as a friend. We know each other from City College," Ellen said. "I asked him to come out for a couple of days and stay in the house over the July 4th weekend."

Abbie told Ellen about Marty and how they were on again, off again.

"Since I moved to New York, I have only been with him, except when we broke up for six months. I thought the relationship was dead, but then he called me unexpectedly and we got back together," Abbie said.

"I guess you are out there looking, just in case. I think you'll have an exciting time in the Hamptons."

Abbie's first weekend in Amagansett was the 4th of July and she invited Marty to drive out as her guest. *I may be defeating the purpose, but Ellen is inviting a guy friend, so maybe that's what people do.*

On Marty's drive out to the Hamptons on the Long Island Expressway, he got a flat tire as he drove past LaGuardia Airport. He never made it out that weekend and Abbie's destiny changed forever.

Chapter Twelve
Summer 1967

For much of the July 4th weekend, the weather was cold and rainy. Housemates and their guests mingled in the living room of the newly constructed cedar house designed with cathedral ceilings and an expansive wood deck that overlooked acres of dazzling white sandy dunes in Amagansett, just past East Hampton.

People talked about how the early summer months in the Hamptons could be so cold and damp that logs were lit and burning strongly in the grand stone fireplace. The spacious main room was packed with women wearing sweatshirts and sweaters over lace knit tops and tight white jeans or capris. Men were in fitted tee shirts and tanks, with black dungarees or canvas shorts. Through the enormous picture window, they could see the path to the beach and marine blue waters of the Atlantic.

In 1967, the beach area in Amagansett, known as the dunes, was just beginning to develop. There were a few scattered houses built and others in construction.

Abbie's new friend Ellen explained that the Village of Amagansett was one town past the more fashionable East Hampton where the singles' action was sizzling. In the dunes, you could still count the number of houses on two hands. The area would eventually become overcrowded with cedar-covered beach houses, on top of one another.

The sky clouded up; rain pounded against the shingled roof, creating a perfect excuse for a big afternoon party. Across the room, Abbie saw Ellen in a filmy white shift over her floral bathing suit. She was standing close by her friend, the man who she said had no romantic interest in her. He was tanned with broad shoulders and thick, dark-brown wavy hair, a bit too long in the back and slightly curled up. A receding hairline accentuated his high forehead.

He doesn't seem to be Ellen's type. Abbie wondered what made him seem so different. As she watched, he walked across the room, through the clusters of people and came close to her.

He spoke carefully, directly to her. His intensely shaded eyes with thick lashes were directed to her alone. "Hi, my name is Samuel. I was born in Russia."

His offbeat look, the trace of an accent, and his shadowy beard intrigued Abbie. His hazel eyes were striking and penetrating.

The Russian didn't bother with small talk. He was direct in telling her he had been born in a labor camp during World War II. His parents had run away from Vilna, their hometown in Poland, and traveled east to Russia where they were arrested and forced into a labor camp in Siberia. That's where Sam was born.

Within the space of five minutes, he told her how they had barely survived and after the seemingly unending war, they were released by the Russians. The family finally made it to the United States in 1949. Sam was still living at home in Whitestone along with a younger sister.

"How about you?" Sam asked.

"Nothing quite as exciting. I'm from Chicago. I'm a teacher. I've never been to the Hamptons before yesterday. Never been to Russia, either, but I am going to Europe this summer."

"Nice. Let's catch up later. There's a party tonight, if the weather clears up."

Later that day, Abbie went to the party with her housemate Jessica, a well-spoken redhead from Queens in her last year of college at George Washington University. Her best friend at school was Lynda Bird Johnson, daughter of the president of the United States. Jessica never talked about it, but everyone knew.

As they were parking in a graveled lot, Abbie saw Samuel getting out of Ellen's car. He had slicked back his wavy dark hair and wore a long-sleeved, light-blue shirt, rolled up at the cuffs and open at the neck. He was wearing extreme cut-off jeans, torn and distressed. His face was a deep tan from the afternoon sunburst. He waved to Abbie and Ellen glanced at her oddly.

Sam didn't try to make conversation with Abbie at the party, only once he glanced her way with an intense stare. He seemed attentive to Ellen and later everyone went to the beach for a marshmallow roast. Some of the guests wandered away in couples and others exhausted like Abbie went to sleep.

"The weekend was better than I expected," she told her roommate Debbie on Sunday night when she returned to the city. "I met this guy who was kind of gorgeous, but he had an odd way of speaking."

"Did he take your number?" Debbie asked.

"No, but it doesn't matter. I'm leaving for Europe next week and won't be in the Hamptons again until August."

Chapter Thirteen

Abbie and Phyllis hugged each other good-bye at JFK baggage claim. They were drained from three action-packed weeks in Europe filled with cathedrals, museums, and statues. And men they encountered across the continent.

"We had an incredible trip. Can you believe that train ride from Amsterdam to Paris?" Abbie said.

"It was the best trip of my life," Phyllis said. "Don't tell anyone how I made out with that perfect stranger in the private compartment on the train. Where were we, anyway?"

"Don't tell anyone about what I did in Lucerne with Hans. After meeting his sister and her husband, I was ready to marry him," Abbie said. "And what about the spaghetti Bolognese on the trains in Italy?"

They said farewell as each went their separate ways. Abbie had to get ready for her new job and Phyllis was going to her mother's place in New Jersey.

The trip really took my mind away from Marty, the on again, off again boyfriend who proposed to me. But where's the ring?

Abbie's memories were blurry after the whirlwind trip. *I vaguely remember a charismatic new man in the Hamptons. He was dark and handsome, somewhat detached at the share house party.*

The cab from the airport dropped her off at her apartment. With her roommates away, it was empty. After setting down her bulging knapsack, she called her mother.

"I'm home safe, Mom," she said. "We had an incredible trip."

"Oh honey, you must be very tired. What are you doing today?"

"I'm getting ready for school to start. You know, I took a new job with New York City Schools. I have two more weekends left on my share in the Hamptons house."

"Well, that should be fun. Are you in touch with Marty or is that over and done with?"

"I don't expect to see him again."

Mother and daughter hung up.

Abbie turned her attention to the television in the living room. *Let's see if there's any news.*

Albert Shanker, head of the New York City teachers' union, was at a podium making an announcement in front of a crowd.

"I am asking all New York City teachers to honor a boycott until a contract settlement passes with the union," Shanker said. "Until our demands are met, we are calling for a strike.

"It's 1967, and it's time we got better pay and better working conditions. I have directed the United Federation of Teachers to vote for a strike."

Abbie listened intently to the announcement. *If schools are closed, I won't have a job. I spent all my savings on the trip to Europe.*

The phone in the front hall rang. Annoyed by the interruption, she answered after the third ring.

"Hi, Abbie?" It was an unfamiliar voice. "This is Sam…you remember, Sam Cooperman…we met at the house in Amagansett. In the Hamptons, remember? I'm Ellen's friend."

There's a teacher's strike. It's no time for a conversation.

Stunned and surprised, she cut him off abruptly. "Hi, Sam. Oh sure, how are you? Listen, I'm watching TV. The teachers' union is announcing a strike. I can't really talk right now. Would you mind calling me later?"

I never gave this guy my phone number. She did recall his slight accent. *Oh yeah, he was born in Russia or someplace in Europe. His family was from Poland. He didn't want anyone to forget that.*

"I'm sorry to interrupt you. Sure, talk to you later," Sam said.

Her mind drifted to the strike.

I'm not even in the teachers' union. Does a strike mean if I want to work, I have to cross a picket line at my school on 23rd Street?

She sat alone in the living room eyes and ears glued to the news on TV.

About 30 minutes later, the phone rang again.

"Who's that?"

Sam had not been deterred by her brushoff.

This guy is persistent.

"Hi, again. Sorry to hear about the strike," Sam said. "I'm going to be in the city tomorrow on business and thought we might get together for dinner."

"Oh," Abbie said. She thought for a moment. "Well, you are a friend of Ellen's and I know how much she likes you, so I don't think we should go out."

Sam replied earnestly, "Honestly, Ellen and I are just friends, and that's all."

Silently, Abbie considered this. She knew it to be true. Ellen had told her that she was crazy about him, but that they were only friends…that he had no romantic interest in her.

Finally, Abbie spoke, "Well, all right. Ellen did tell me you two are friends. I can make it on Monday night, tomorrow."

"I'll pick you up at 7 then," Sam said.

She gave him her address.

All she could think of, besides the teacher's strike, was that she had nothing to wear, and definitely, no cute shoes. Sam had mentioned he was in the garment business or maybe shoes, something like that. So, she borrowed a little lime green print polyester shirtwaist dress from her roommate and some adorable white flats. When she opened the door the next evening, Sam was standing there with a big smile on his face. His next glance went right to her feet.

Chapter Fourteen
Sam

Sam and his family were survivors of the Holocaust. His parents and grandparents, aunts and uncles, were from Vilna, Poland. In 1939, Hitler invaded Poland with determined, dark plans to exterminate the Polish Jews. Sam's mother, Sophia Ruskin, was a member of a well-to-do family that owned a knitting factory. They were not religious and considered themselves to be ardent Poles. Manny Cooperman, Sam's father, was from a more modest family background; his domineering mother urged him to marry up. He was tall and handsome, with a charming smile and a sparkle in his hazel eyes.

When the war in Europe broke out, many Jews considered running away, but they didn't have a definite destination. In 1940, one year before Hitler commenced the extermination program, Stalin ordered the deportation of about 200,000 Polish Jews from Russian-occupied Eastern Poland to Gulag labor camps buried deep in the Soviet Union. Inadvertently, Stalin's vicious order saved these Jewish lives.

In 1941, Russia and Germany established a peace accord. Between 1940-1941, many Jews fled Poland of their own accord, at significant risk. They had no legitimate documents enabling them to cross the border to Russia and were easily arrested. Those who were not executed on the spot were shipped to labor camps and forced to work as near-slaves. They barely survived in appalling conditions in Siberia, compelled to work long back-breaking hours in bitterly freezing weather with only scraps of inferior food.

As conditions grew worse in Poland, Sophia's father approached Manny and asked him to marry his daughter and take her to safety. Manny's sister had already been able to get out and sail to the United States. Sophia's brothers had been rounded up and sent to concentration camps.

Nobody guessed that Germany would attack Russia in 1941 and that bloody war would ensue on that front. It was widely believed that the war would last only a few years and the horror would end, allowing everyone to return to their normal lives in Poland. In Manny's mind, the marriage he agreed to was essentially a wartime arrangement. When life went back to normal, the marriage could be annulled.

After a simple wedding ceremony in one of the remaining synagogues in Vilna, the newlyweds packed up a few belongings, kissed their parents and remaining relatives a sad good-bye and fled east to Russia, the former Soviet Union. They hoped that one day they would be together again.

Like other refugees, they were captured and banished to Siberia. It was here that Sam was born at the end of 1942 in a refugee camp. His mother lingered for months with a fever after childbirth, and Sam barely survived.

It was an astounding miracle that the newly married Sophia and Manny Cooperman escaped Hitler's extermination of the Jews in Poland. Another miracle followed, then another: Sam was born, and they survived the horrible camp in Siberia. By the end of the war in 1945, most of the refugees in the camps had perished but Sam, Sophia, and Manny made it through the horror. Little Sam was taught to beg for scraps of food, and Manny bartered for medicine on the black market when Sam nearly died from a bout with diphtheria, and when his mother's infection lingered.

After the war the ravenous family somehow made their way back to devastated Poland where almost 99 percent of the Jews had been murdered. None of their relatives had survived except for two cousins who worked for Oscar Schindler, and the sister who got away and made the journey to America. Now the family went west to a displaced persons camp in Germany. Sam's sister was born there.

When Manny had volunteered to flee Poland and take Sophia to safety, no one expected the war would last more than five years. But now that the war was finally over in 1945, he had a family to raise and fate had changed his life forever. After two years in Germany, HIAS, a dominant Jewish agency of the time, arranged for the family's passage to the United States where they were to be settled in Northern California. But when they arrived in New York, Manny's surviving sister Sara begged them to stay. The refugee agency informed them that if they stayed in New York, they were on their own, and they agreed to the conditions.

Little Sam became the rock of the family and as he grew up, he vowed to work hard and take care of his family. Survival was the only thing he knew. The main thing he learned from growing up in a labor camp and later a camp for displaced persons was to hold onto things. To hide money and gold and anything of value that he earned from his hard work.

Chapter Fifteen

On her first date with Sam, Abbie wore a borrowed polyester print dress and cute white flats. The young man was wearing a light blue shirt, open at the neck, and a pair of tan chino pants with a brown leather belt. He had on Gucci loafers, no socks. His wavy black hair was combed back highlighting his cheekbones and brilliant hazel eyes.

"Do you like hamburgers and fries? Let's walk over to Daly's Dandelion," Sam suggested, standing in front of Abbie's building on 70th Street near Second Avenue.

"Do you think we can get a table?" Abbie asked. "It's usually pretty crowded."

"It's a Monday, so there shouldn't be much of a problem. Anyway, I know a guy who works there."

As soon as she walked in, Abbie thought, "This reminds me of Friday's."

The casual bar and grill, a popular hangout on First Avenue, had a cavernous feel. Like Friday's, it was decorated with checkered tablecloths and art deco lighting fixtures. The walls were painted red with white trim moldings.

The place was already crowded, but they were ushered to a comfortable table near the center of the room. A young waiter quickly came over and handed them menus.

"Would you like drinks?" he asked.

"Yes, I'll have a glass of the house red wine," Sam said.

"Water for me, please," Abbie said. "I think I would like a diet coke, also."

Nearby two other couples were talking about birthdays. They were laughing and joking around.

The waiter appeared with a decorated cake with blazing candles. He set it down in front of a woman with blonde hair tied back in a ponytail.

"Happy Birthday to you, Happy Birthday to you," the group sang, slightly off key. Abbie and Sam joined them in celebrating.

The woman blowing out the candles looked towards Abbie and Sam. "It's my birthday. I'm 40 years old," she said.

"You don't look like 40," Abbie said. *What a beautiful woman.*

"It comes sooner than you think." She paused and looked at them with interest. "Have you two known each other a long time?"

"No, it's our first date," Sam answered. "We just figured out that we have the same birthday two years apart."

The other dark-haired woman said, "That's unbelievable. Your first date and you have the same birthday."

The birthday lady said, "That's an omen. You two are going to get married. What's your sign?"

Sam smiled. Abbie giggled.

"We're both Capricorns," she said. "It's funny that we have the same birthday."

"My parents are never sure what day I was actually born. The war was going on and they were stuck in a labor camp," Sam said.

"What happened to your family after the war?" Abbie asked.

"It's a long story, but we finally got to the U.S. near family that had gotten out early. We didn't speak any English. My sister was only about two years old."

"It must have been hard for you," Abbie said.

"Yes, and my parents have never gotten over it. They ran from Poland thinking it would be temporary. Ended up in Siberia where the Russians took refugees from Eastern Europe. "I almost died from starvation and diphtheria."

At that point, Sam trailed off. Abbie could tell he didn't want to talk about it.

She shifted the subject to his business. The family owned a shoe store and that's how Sam had gotten interested in manufacturing footwear.

"By the way, I really like your shoes," Sam said. "You have a narrow foot."

"Thanks, I do wear a narrow size. These are really comfortable."

After dinner and coffee, they walked up Second Avenue to Abbie's apartment building. When they crossed the street at 68th and Second, Sam took her hand.

In front of her building, Sam put his hands on her shoulders and bent to kiss her. He walked her inside to the elevator, and said softly, "I had a lovely evening."

She quickly licked her lips and moved towards him. The connection was utterly natural. One more time he pressed his perfect full lips to hers for a tender moment. Then he looked at her thoughtfully.

"Goodnight, pleasant dreams."

Breathless, Abbie went up in the elevator to her apartment and opened the door.

Good, no one's home.

She went to the window to see if she could see Sam. He was looking back at her building.

The next day, he called and asked her out again.

"Are you busy Saturday night? Would you like to go out for dinner?"

"Yes, I would love to," Abbie said.

"I'll pick you up at 6. Is that okay? We'll go to Little Italy. I know a really great place that you will like a lot."

Chapter Sixteen

Abbie worried about what she would wear, as usual. She was very excited about her second date with Sam.

She told Debbie about her date. "It was kind of magical. We're going out again."

"What about Marty? Are you done with him?"

"I'm going to have to make some kind of excuse until I figure this out."

On their second date, Sam took Abbie to Teddy's, an old-style Italian restaurant downtown. It was dim inside with black velvet walls and chunky white candles lit on every table.

Sam ordered a bottle of Chianti and shrimp cocktail for two. After the first glass of wine, Abbie couldn't see straight. Sam squeezed her thigh under the table. She felt light-headed, and almost let out a moan.

After a dinner of veal parmigiana and spaghetti, they were stuffed.

"Let's walk around Little Italy for a while," Sam said.

People were sitting outside cafes sipping tiny cups of expresso and eating pastries and gelato.

Back in the car, Sam said, "I'm temporarily staying with my parents in Whitestone. It's not what I would like, but for now, it's fine. I'll be going away on business in a few weeks. Would you like to see where we live? My parents are probably sleeping."

Abbie agreed. They drove uptown and over the bridge until they came to a quiet residential part of Queens near water. They parked in front of a modest red brick townhouse where Sam led her into the lower level. It seemed to be a finished basement apartment with a couch and a double sized bed covered with a plaid quilt. On the couch, they talked quietly about the evening and then Sam ran upstairs to see if his folks were sleeping.

Sam reached for her and drew her close to him. Abbie was nervous about his parents upstairs, but she tried to relax and went along with his romantic advances.

His kisses grew passionate and he ran his hand across her breasts slowly pressing them as he moved. She could smell aftershave cologne on his rough cheek. He helped her undo her bra and take off her tights.

Her breath was coming in little gasps and she could feel herself grow wet with desire.

He's going to think I'm a slut. I guess I am, but it feels so right to be here with him. I'm falling for him.

Marty's face flashed in her mind, but she shut it out.

After the intimacy, she pulled herself together, fixing her hair and arranging her clothes on her spent body.

Sam drove her home about 1 a.m. He held her a long time at the door. She didn't want to let him go.

The next afternoon, Abbie called Marty. She wasn't sure what to say but she had to end the relationship, and she had to do it now.

At least, I have to put it on hold. I'll tell him the truth.

"I've met someone else and I can't see you for a while," she said.

"Honey, what are you saying? I-I-I don't get it," Who did you meet? When did this happen?"

Abbie was adamant. She was done with him. She carefully put the phone in its cradle.

Chapter Seventeen

After their dinner date and passionate tryst in his parents' house, Abbie began to see Sam several nights a week. She had never dated a businessman before.

Summer had turned into autumn. Sam invited her to come to an industry shoe show at the Waldorf Astoria Hotel. He was meeting with business associates about his new line of footwear.

"I'm going to manufacture shoes in Taiwan," Sam said. "Several factories are already lined up to copy shoe samples I'll be bringing them."

"I'm not sure exactly what he does," Abbie mentioned to her roommate, Debbie. "One thing for certain though is when he talks about his business, his face lights up."

Abbie had noticed that Sam had a unique way of talking, and not just his accent. "He looks you squarely in the eye, and makes you feel like the only person in the world who matters."

She thought about Marty, who was talkative and bombastic, an all-American athlete, and not like Sam at all.

Sam was charming, serious, and enigmatic. He loved fine dining and they made the rounds of every gourmet restaurant in the city. But he liked deli, too. One night, the couple went walking on Second Avenue after a meal of corned beef sandwiches and French fries.

Years later, Abbie remembered that night because much later Sam would embrace organic juicing, sprouts, and homeopathic medicine potions. But in 1967, corned beef with mustard was still a favorite with the fries.

They stopped in front of a shoe store window that night to look at the merchandise. Sam always had an eye out for new fashions.

He took out his business card from a pocket and showed it to Abbie. "I'm going to be very successful."

Standing in front of a familiar pizza place, he put his arm around her and kissed the top of her head. When she looked up, he pressed his lips to hers and held her close. She felt his heart pounding against her own.

When people asked later why she married him so quickly, she recalled their first date and those that followed. "He was sure of himself, so charming and so self-confident. He literally swept me off my feet."

During their third week of dating, she cooked dinner for him at her apartment when the roommates were out. The lease was expiring soon, once again, and they were all trying to find new places to live. She was tired of the Upper East Side and had started to look downtown for a studio apartment.

For dinner that evening, Abbie roasted baby Cornish hens stuffed with wild rice. She had never made them before but decided to try a recipe she had found in *Ladies Home Journal.*

She made a green salad with small cucumbers and cherry tomatoes and a vinaigrette dressing that Yvette concocted. The little pine table was set with cloth napkins and she used the only two crystal goblets in the house for rose wine.

Sam was surprised that she could cook and devoured every bit of food, neatly wiping the corners of his mouth.

"You didn't tell me you could cook," he said. They sipped wine and laughed. "You can really cook. This is delicious."

Then, sitting there in the front hall, Sam lifted his glass, looked intensely into Abbie's eyes and said, "Will you marry me?"

Abbie's felt her heart stop. For several moments, she was silent.

"Sam, you are crazy," she burst out. "We've only known each other for 21 days."

"So, what! I haven't been counting," he said laughing.

Then, he reminded her that he was going on a business trip to the Far East.

"Are you really?" she asked, her voice high pitched. "How long will you be gone?"

"I'm meeting with a Japanese company about a joint venture," he said. "It's a big deal that could finance my import business."

"I promise I will write, don't worry, and we will make plans," he said in a serious tone. "You will come with me on the next trip. I promise, my darling."

After Sam left, Abbie collapsed on her bed. *This can't actually be happening.*

Sam wasn't joking because his family started to call Abbie, wanting to meet her. They planned to marry that December, because his sister was engaged and already had her own wedding arranged at a banquet hall in Larchmont.

She waited a week and then on a Sunday, Abbie called her parents, excited to tell them that Sam, this new man in her life, had proposed to her.

In her typical negative voice, her mother objected to the whole scenario. "You always believe everything that everyone says to you. It's too soon to know."

"This guy means it." *I won't let you deter me. I'm not going to take your negative comments to heart.*

Over the next couple of months, Sam flew to Japan and Taipei where he was getting his new venture off the ground. Any doubts about the seriousness of his proposal of marriage were dispelled by calls from his family.

His sister, Rachel, came to meet Abbie, who had moved to 38th Street between Third Avenue and Lexington. She had a new roommate who was almost never home. Andrea, a buyer for Bradley's department store chain, was either with her boyfriend or working.

Sam's absence seemed to go on forever, but Abbie was teaching and planning their small wedding with the help of her future mother-in-law, sweet Sophia. She and Abbie had felt connected from their first meeting.

In fact, Abbie had met the whole family, including aunts, uncles, and cousins, making her feel like she belonged. Even Manny, Sam's stern and stately handsome father, showered her with hugs and beaming smiles.

Despite the attention from Sam's family, she felt alone in her new apartment in an unfamiliar neighborhood. Change had come quickly, leaving her anxious and uncertain.

Still, Abbie smiled and went with Sophia to the wedding reception hall to make the actual arrangements for December 28, their wedding date. Sophia, slightly bent in posture, but determined, knew her way around town. In the Bronx they shopped for simple and inexpensive wedding dresses at Loehmann's and at other small bridal shops.

It was at Alexander's department store on Fordham Road that Abbie found a pretty, lacy white dress that came to her knees. At age 23, almost 24, she wore a size 7.

The one thing she knew for sure was that she would have to buy beautiful shoes, no matter what the cost. After purchasing a wedding dress at a budget department store, she spent $150 for stunning white satin low-heeled pumps at a Madison Avenue boutique.

Chapter Eighteen

Sam left for the Far East in late October with a promise to return in three weeks. Before he departed, he talked about his plans for their future.

"This business is for my family and for our future,"

"Three weeks is a long time," Abbie said. "You may forget about me so far away."

"Next trip, you will go with me."

Before leaving, they enjoyed one more romantic dinner at a quiet bistro in Greenwich Village where they mostly held hands and stared at each other.

"When I come home, we should go to Chicago for a weekend so I can meet your family, so they won't be strangers at our wedding," Sam said.

"I'll make some plans and reservations. One more thing, will you write to me?"

"I'll try." Then they parted reluctantly, kissing one more time.

He's such a good kisser. She sighed as she let herself into her empty apartment. It was sparsely furnished and dim. There was a small lamp by her twin-size bed and a standing lamp in the corner. The kitchen was tiny and old-fashioned. Steeling herself for the coming weeks, she set to work on doing lesson plans for her new students thinking about the short distance she was from the school where she was now teaching. She could make it in twenty minutes on foot.

About a week after Sam departed, letters started to arrive. Almost every day, she received a love letter written in a flourishing hand from her future husband. The flurry of letters written on crisp, semitransparent hotel stationary always began with, "Darling Abbie…" Sam kept her up to date with details about Japan and Taipei.

He wrote, "The factories are working on shoe samples. If only they could get it right. Then I could come home sooner. I miss you so."

His flowing penmanship and romantic words were more than she had ever expected from a businessman. One pleasing note was, "I promise to buy you a jade engagement ring in Hong Kong on a future trip."

Keeping busy during his absence was not a problem. Abbie concentrated on her new teaching job.

She dreaded crossing the picket line during the teachers strike. Although she sympathized with the teachers, this was her first assignment with New York City, and she was not a member of their tightly run union.

Every night, she thought about Sam, remembering how he held her hand walking in the city. Falling asleep at night, she recounted his tender moments and affectations when they were alone. She appreciated his commitment and references to their future, something she had never gotten from Marty.

She resisted thoughts of Marty, her reason for staying in New York. She remembered their first wildly passionate night together in his walk-up studio. That experience, a week before she was going to leave for home, had prompted her to call Teachers College about the fellowship that might be waiting for her.

Marty had become her best friend and support system. She missed not talking to him every day, not hearing that breezy, chipper voice, but that was over.

She had gotten that college fellowship and moved on to a new life. Marty, for whatever reason she would not know for many years, had broken his devotion to her.

Sam was the serious man in her life, the man who would put a ring on her finger. A gold wedding band. Then later a jade ring, maybe.

Sam's sister Rachel called Abbie and came to visit several times to inspect her new downtown apartment, telling her stories about the Cooperman family and their miraculous escape from war-torn Europe. As refugees in America, her parents had peddled second-hand dry goods on seedy streets in the South Bronx.

Abbie warmed easily to vivacious Rachel who resembled Sam in coloring and features. She rattled on proudly about her mother, Sophia, an expert seamstress who repaired remnants of used clothes. Manny, the patriarch of the family, dealt with customers bargaining for materials and goods.

Rachel's eyes lit up when she talked about Sam. When Sam was only ten years old, he took care of Rachel and walked her to and from kindergarten.

On her several visits, it was obvious that Rachel was assessing Abbie to see if she would fit into the tight-knit clan. The young women had lunch together at the coffee shop on the corner. She confided in Abbie about her own fiancée's quirks and how excited she was about getting married.

By the time Sam returned from the Far East, Abbie had become close to the entire family, including cousins Shana and Walter and Sam's Aunt Sara, his father's only surviving sibling. They sat around on many nights in their cozy living room in Whitestone reminiscing about the war, how they had run away from Hitler's SS troops when they invaded Poland, and about all the relatives that had perished in concentration camps.

One night, cousin Shana said, "Walter and I survived the war years working for a factory owner who employed husbands and wives. He kept us together."

Abbie said, "Really. How did he do that?"

Shana said, "We don't know. Somehow, we got through the war years without being sent to a camp."

Three weeks went by and still no Sam. After six weeks, Sam finally came home, a few weeks before their wedding. He looked exhausted and drained.

"It was a struggle from start to finish, but some products are coming in next week, which I can start selling."

He rested, sleeping two long nights, before they left for Chicago. Abbie was nervous about how her parents would behave. She worried about where they would take Sam to dinner in downtown Chicago. It had to be nice but not overly expensive. They decided on tasteful Armando's, a classic Italian restaurant with tablecloths, but a friendly atmosphere.

Those were the details that concerned Abbie. Her father drove them downtown and dinner went without incident from Abbie's sassy mother.

On Sunday, Sam got to meet her whole family at her sister's suburban house where they hosted an engagement party. Sam was elegant and friendly, getting along especially well with Abbie's young nieces.

Abbie's best friend, Roz, came. She thought that Sam was gorgeous. Everything about the visit went perfectly fine. No major upsets or recriminations from Bessie. *What a relief.*

And the marriage was changing from fantasy to reality. She was going to have a husband. It may have been someone she hardly knew…someone she was still getting to know…but doesn't that happen with many girls? You meet someone, there's chemistry, and you take a chance.

If you want to go forward, you have to take a leap of faith. But at night, in bed, she had panic attacks, tossing and turning. In the morning, her hair was damp on the pillow.

"Should I marry him? Abbie asked Lisa, one of her young nieces. "It sounds crazy, but I don't know what to do."

"It's like a fairy tale," Lisa said. "He's so handsome and he has that cute accent."

On the day of their wedding, a massive blizzard blew in threatening the drive from the city to the banquet hall in Larchmont. That morning, Abbie had gone to a neighborhood beauty salon in Manhattan to get her hair done up in a French twist. She was stressed and nervous as a lonesome kitten. A cold draft was blowing on her wet head. To make matters worse, her mother was angry at Abbie.

"I feel like a stranger," Bessie said. "Why do you have to get married in New York?

"I don't trust these people. They are different from us because of what they went through," she went on. "Where are they getting all of their money? Why does Sam do business in China?"

"Mother, it's Taiwan, not China. Can't you give me some support on this happy occasion?"

Abbie cringed at her mother's aggravating assaults.

No wonder I moved a thousand miles away from her.

It was a small, but lovely wedding with about 70 guests, including family, friends, and business associates. For their wedding night, Sam had reserved a suite at the posh Plaza Hotel. Abbie suffered from a miserably heavy cold, triggered by the pressure and anxiety of getting married, and the stress caused by her mother's disapproval and admonitions.

On New Year's Day, Sam left Abbie alone at the hotel near Central Park while he went to Boston for a business meeting with a wholesaler. It was the fourth day of their marriage. There would be many more days like that, and weeks, when he was away on business. And many more lavish hotel suites, all over the world.

Abbie called her mother. "Sam went to a business meeting. I'm alone with a dripping nose and cough."

Bessie said, "It's okay, sweetheart. It will work out."

Abbie was pleased by her mother's reassurance.

"I know. I love him and tomorrow we leave on our honeymoon."

Chapter Nineteen

Less than a week after their hurriedly planned wedding, Abbie and Sam left for the Far East on a combination business trip and honeymoon. Abbie placed her passport in her carry-on bag and made sure she had her lipstick and tissues for the six-hour flight to San Francisco.

Sam packed his passport in his briefcase with some documents he wanted to review on the plane. Manny drove the couple to JFK where they were taking TWA non-stop. At the gate, Manny said good-bye to his son and to his new daughter-in-law.

With tears in his eyes, he said, "I wish you both to be well and to have a successful trip. The family will miss you. Call us every week, if you can. Let us know how things are going." He gave an affectionate hug to Abbie. Then he took Sam by the shoulders and kissed him roughly on each cheek.

Abbie was excited thinking about their first flight together. The newlyweds checked in at the TWA counter with two suitcases. Sam kept touching his worn-looking brown leather briefcase.

"It brings me luck," Sam told Abbie.

On the luxurious plane, the couple sat side by side in comfortable seats in the tenth row before the first exit. They talked for a while and then watched a movie. The stewardess dressed in a navy-blue skirt and white blouse served a hot lunch in a small white tray. Sam wouldn't touch it, but Abbie was hungry.

As they approached San Francisco, they gazed at the magnificent bay and the Golden Gate Bridge.

"Have you ever seen such a gorgeous view?" Abbie said.

"It's one of my favorite cities," Sam said. "There's a free-spirited feeling compared to buttoned up New York City."

They had gained time traveling west and after checking into the Marriott Hotel on Market Street, they wandered around until dark. They toured the Mission district, munching on spicy chicken burritos, wandered around the ports at Embarcadero, and had a taxi drive them through the Haight-Ashbury district where the hippie culture thrived.

"I guess this is what you meant about free spirits. Maybe we should get some beads and a guitar and hang out with the hippies," Abbie said.

Sam looked at her like she was crazy. "You know, they are anti-establishment."

Exhausted they went back to their hotel and fell asleep. In the morning, they could do whatever they wanted. No business meetings or phone calls.

"Let's go to Sausalito," Sam suggested. "It is the southernmost part of Marin County."

They took the ferry across the bay to Sausalito for lunch, eating stuffed clams and baked scallops in garlic sauce. They strolled along the deep blue harbor, remembering funny things about their intimate wedding and the business that lay ahead of them.

"My mother was driving me crazy," Abbie said.

"My father was making me nervous. We both come from difficult parents."

Abbie was learning about the man she married. She saw women notice him, his bold looks enhanced by his suave demeanor, like a movie idol in a Hollywood classic. Every night in bed, Sam made love to her. The first few nights were an awakening. She couldn't help but compare him to Marty.

He is not as tender as Marty. He's not playful, and kind of rough and silent. But Marty never satisfied me either and when we talked about it, he said it was my fault.

After two days in San Francisco, they left for Honolulu, the main island of Hawaii. That was designated as their actual honeymoon.

One night at a luau at the Honolulu Hilton, Sam opened-up about his business goals. "I already told you about how a guy I know in the shoe business became the largest importer of shoes out of Taiwan."

"He ended up selling his company to a conglomerate for $60 million and now he's retired. I want to be the next big importer and retire by the time I'm 50.

"Will you help me? There's some work you could do."

It turned out he meant keeping track of orders and expenses. Abbie felt flattered that he needed her, counted on her.

"Yes, I'd be glad to. When we get to Taipei, maybe the hotel will let me use a typewriter."

Their four-day stay in Hawaii was spent at the beach and roaming around the island.

"It's pretty here, but touristy," said Abbie.

"It will be much more exotic and exciting in Japan and Taipei. I hope you realize we'll be gone for a month or more."

"I love adventure." Saying that startled her.

In Honolulu, they did a lot of shopping. Sam was always looking for stylish shoes that he could copy for a lower price market.

One afternoon after a lunch of conch chowder, they stopped in a Hawaiian theme boutique. There were lots of cotton dresses, but also more sophisticated outfits.

"This would look good on you," he said, pulling it from the rack.

Abbie had not gotten a new dress in a long time. She tried on a mustard yellow knit mini-dress and some black leather pumps with a bow on each toe.

"Darling," he stroked her hair and chuckled. "You are the girl of my dreams. We are going to have a beautiful family and good fortune."

Abbie, a smart girl, though shy and reserved, had found her true love. It turned out that Sam had a similar temperament. Everyone said, "They are the perfect couple."

Chapter Twenty

When Abbie and Sam landed in Tokyo, the airport was madness, people and uniformed guards everywhere. All arriving passengers had to go through customs, a serious business, judging by the look on the officials' faces.

A tall, slim customs agent, in a gray uniform, had a thin black mustache and eyebrows that were too close to his eyes. He motioned them over to his station, looking at them sternly as he checked their bags.

"Do you have any swords or rapiers?" he asked. He included the "w" sound when he said "swords" and he didn't take his flashing eyes off of them.

Abbie had trouble keeping a straight face.

"Pardon me?" said Sam. Not meaning to be flip.

The customs officer repeated, "Do you have any swords or rapiers?"

He asked the same question of Abbie. She tried not to giggle.

"No," said Sam.

"No," said Abbie.

Finally, he let them proceed past the customs inspection area.

When they got to the curb for a taxi, Abbie was struck by the urban chaos.

"It's always this way," Sam said. "Tokyo is the busiest and noisiest city in the Far East. It makes Manhattan seem quiet."

After a long ride through heavy traffic and monstrous horn honking, they reached the Palace Hotel. The hotel, erected in the late 1950s, was palatial and ultra-modern. Their huge room was decorated in shades of ivory and blue.

"I'm exhausted. How about you?" said Sam. "Let's take a nap. We're having dinner tonight with my joint venture partners."

"Mr. Matsumoto may bring his wife, but probably not. They don't really socialize that much with their wives, except for private family affairs."

Soon after hanging up her clothes, Abbie decided to skip a nap. She put on some slacks and a sweater and went to the beauty salon in the hotel gallery where the attendants pampered her. They washed and dried her hair, massaged her neck and back, manicured her nails, all the time chattering to each other, repeating *kawaidesu, kawaidesu…* Pretty, pretty…

Later in the modern dining room, Abbie and Sam met the business partners. Besides Mr. Matsumoto, an unusually tall man, there were three other men in identical business suits, white shirts and black ties. They were much shorter and less outgoing than their boss.

They each stood stiffly and bowed from the waist. "Good evening," they said in stilted English. "Good evening." Then in Japanese, "Konichi wa."

Sam responded, "Konichi wa. It is good to see you all."

Abbie nodded but was tongue tied. She was the only woman at the table and the only American woman in the dining room.

The waiter poured warm sake in small ceramic cups and the men sipped it, toasting Sam. They had two rounds of sake.

Every sip of wine was accompanied by a hearty "Compai, Compai," the traditional Japanese toast. Then scotch was ordered and poured on glasses with ice.

Mr. Matsumoto turned to Abbie and asked, "How do you like Tokyo?"

The other gentlemen spoke no English, but they kept nodding and smiling at Abbie.

"It's a wonderful city and I'm so happy to be here," she said, smiling sweetly.

"One evening you will get to meet Mrs. Matsumoto," said Mr. Matsumoto.

"I would love to meet your wife," said Abbie.

Dinner was ordered. The men all ordered Kobe beef, browned potatoes that looked roasted, and steamed vegetables. Abbie had filet of sole stuffed with shrimp in white wine butter sauce and sticky rice.

Abbie wrote in her diary

> I could tell Sam was a little bit anxious, but he pulled it off. The men were excited to finance his venture. Another thing I noticed about my husband. He is a very picky eater. If he doesn't get what he wants, like the French fries he ordered, he gets short-tempered and annoyed. Oh, well, take the good with the bad.

Abbie and Sam spent two more days in Tokyo. Every day, she found out new things about Sam.

One night at dinner by themselves, he said, "I love the way you move. You are my awkward little girl."

"What do you mean?"

"You are lovely in ways I've never seen in other women. Soft, but also tentative. Confident, but a little shy and sweet."

In the light of Sam's attention and adoration, Abbie began to feel more at ease and comfortable

Marty disappointed me, but now I'm married. I have a husband who is devoted to me and has taken me with him to the other side of the world.

Because of Sam, Abbie could still believe in happily ever after. In her heart, she was still that dreamy little girl play acting in her parents' bedroom, cutting pictures from movie star magazines for her scrapbook, and listening to love songs.

Abbie was convinced by now that Sam had a flair for selling and making deals. The way he dressed and maneuvered around the city and now in the Far East was astonishing to her.

He can be shy and awkward like me. She wrote in her diary. *Sometimes he stammers a little talking on the phone to customers. I'm worried that the person on the other end will hang up on him.*

Yet he always knew where to go and what to do. And he was selling and getting purchase orders from wholesalers that sold to Woolworth and K-Mart. Abbie knew because she was typing up the orders on the hotel typewriter.

Chapter Twenty-One

For two weeks, the couple had no contact with their families back home. One night, though, at the hotel, Sam was especially tense and trying to get through to his parents. International calls were placed in advance through an operator who scheduled a time.

"I'm so worried about my parents," Sam said, running his fingers through his thick dark wavy hair.

"My family has always depended on me to take care of things, to protect my little sister, and to be a success. My whole life, since I was a child during the war …. my parents always counted on me."

"I thought your father ran the shoe stores. He seems so capable," Abbie said.

"Yes, he does run the stores, manages the building…for a long time. But he's getting older and the business is not what it used to be. Our customers don't always have money to spend and the rents on our stores are going up."

On the phone, Sam gave his father a report on the business partnership. They always spoke to each other in Polish, so Abbie had to guess what they were saying.

She felt the first inklings of being left out, on the periphery of a tight-knit family who had lived through troubled times. They emigrated to a new country where they had to learn a new language and make a living. His parents were in their late 40s when they had to start their lives over.

"When we first went to the supermarket, we didn't know apple sauce from baby food," Manny always joked.

Abbie realized it was more than a family joke. It was a reminder of the family's new beginnings in a totally different world. A forced exodus after years of grim horror.

The couple's next stop was Kobe. Sam was meeting with partners to check out factories. It was a small friendly city next to Osaka, a well-known port city. They stayed at the Newport Hotel, bustling with Americans and Europeans doing trade agreements and business deals.

One night, they discovered a small Italian restaurant near the harbor. It was owned by an American named Fred Thomas. After he had served in World War II, Fred got stationed in Osaka following the peace treaty. There he met and married a graceful Japanese woman and fell in love. He never returned to his home in Minnesota.

Abbie and Sam were so homesick for Little Italy that they dined at Fred's trattoria every night for seven days straight. There was something about the local ingredients combined with the owner's flair for making sauces and parmigiana dishes and his American-style conversation.

Each night, Fred stopped by their table. "How are my newlyweds doing tonight? Did you enjoy your dinner?"

Kyoshi, his wife, was always there, too. "Good evening, friends. When do you leave for Taipei? We will miss you."

Abbie and Sam promised to come back on their next trip. "You make us feel so at home."

By the time they left Japan, Abbie was in love with the friendly port city.

I'm in love with Sam, too. I can't believe I only met him six months ago in a beach house on the shores of Long Island.

Chapter Twenty-Two

Finally, the couple were on their way to Taipei, their most important destination for business. Sam had plans to stay there for four weeks.

On the plane, Sam cautioned her about the city. "It's big with crowds of people, mostly Taiwanese who settled the island in the last century. Most of the well-to-do people there own the factories and are originally from mainland China."

"Franklin is the factory owner I'm dealing with. He and his wife grew up in Shanghai, then went to college in the U.S. They speak perfect English.

"You will like them. When I'm at work, you are free to go out to lunch and shop around. Go to the museum. People will take you. There are many American businesspeople staying at the President Hotel."

Sam's plan was to stay for several weeks at the hotel while he worked on getting shoe samples designed and manufactured for the U.S. market. Abbie was free to explore the city, at first accompanied by Franklin's wife, who was a beautiful and sophisticated woman.

Soon Abbie became friendly with a waitress who served them at the hotel; her name was Diana and she wanted to practice English. Diana offered to show Abbie around Taipei and teach her some Mandarin.

Many afternoons the hotel workers could see Abbie working on the typewriter in one of their offices.

"How's business?" asked Diana, who was passing by to get her paycheck.

"Good. We're getting some orders for samples. Have you heard of Woolworth?"

Other times, Abbie ventured out alone to observe the locals. She took pictures with her Nikon camera, snapping shots of peasants on river boats. Having ice cream one day, she met a 19-year-old woman whose family owned Bresler's ice cream parlor. Three afternoons a week, they ate ice cream with chocolate sauce, and talked.

Abbie was learning Mandarin, or at least a few words she needed to know. The name for the hotel. How to say, "That's too expensive."

Good night. Pretty girl. It was a beautiful sounding language, with a sing song tone.

One day she asked Sam, "Do you mind if I visit some schools for the deaf? I was invited for lunch by the director of one of the schools."

"Sure, honey. That sounds great. Please just type up those few orders for Kmart.

"Don't forget we are going out for dinner with Franklin and his wife. They are taking us to the Grand Hotel for a banquet.".

"What should I wear? Is it dressy? I imagine so."

"Wear that new dress I bought you at Saks. The periwinkle blue one with the white lacy collar. You're so beautiful in that dress."

Every evening, there was a formal dinner or banquet. She loved the fried rice with vegetables and slivers of roast pork, and Peking duck was always the main delicacy. The waiter would slice it up and make sandwiches topped with hoisin sauce for everyone at the table. There were no forks or knives, just chop sticks and spoons.

In the hotel coffee shop, Abbie longed for a tuna fish sandwich on white bread. *A plain hamburger with pickles from McDonald's would sure taste good too.*

She kept a notebook of things she saw. The taxi drivers racing through the crowded streets. Dilapidated automobiles and reckless drivers. Pedestrians in shabby clothes on foot or on beat up bicycles. Families floating by in sampan boats on the river.

Pressed duck hung in grocery store windows. Peasants eating noodles with their chopsticks. It was impossible to find pastries or cake that were not dry and sandy tasting.

Street sewers were not always covered or contained. The stench of garbage filled the heavy, humid air of this changing city. Once inhabited by peasants and farmers, Taipei had become the seat of the Chinese Nationalist government after the communists took over mainland China.

When she and Sam arrived back in New York, her heart swelled as she said to him, "Isn't it great to be back home?"

They walked down the stairs of the huge plane right onto the tarmac at JFK. She wanted to cry as she bent down and kissed the ground.

Once at home, she thought about Marty. Flashbacks kept filling her mind, unnerving her. What was he doing? She remembered what he said when she called to say she was getting engaged.

"What? Oh, wow. I don't know what to say," Marty had stammered. "I wish you the best."

Chapter Twenty-Three

Shoe samples were strewn over the Oriental rug and dark hardwood floors in the living room on West 72nd Street where Eve, Abbie's 14-month-old daughter, toddled about. The baby picked up a sandal and put a strap in her mouth. Abbie distracted her with a stuffed teddy bear.

The shoes were grouped in categories — slippers, sandals, flats, all manufactured in Taiwan factories. Sam had spent long weeks and months putting samples together to be merchandised to department stores and discount chains, like Woolworth and K-Mart.

Abbie looked back upon those early years in the city when she was pregnant twice and gave birth to Eve and to Lila. She could picture their first apartment. Life was definitely copacetic, as Marty might have said.

We travel a few times a year and entertain, she told Marty in her imagination. *I'm having the time of my life. Sam is high-strung, though, and a bully.*

Sam was under pressure and determined to be financially successful. By 1970, he was earning six figures.

"I want to be a tycoon," he told their friends. "I never want my family to be wanting anything ever again."

In 1969, the couple took one-year-old Eve with them on a business trip to the Far East. Abbie met an American family with the consulate. Barbara and Sidney Davidson opened their home to Abbie on two lengthy stays. After Lila was born, they took both girls and spent three months at the President Hotel in two rooms. Julie, an amah, helped them.

The Davidsons lived on Yangmingshan (Grass Mountain) in the outskirts of Taipei city where many Americans resided during their stays for business or government jobs. They enjoyed special privileges at the Officers Club where you could find American-style hamburgers and hot dogs on buns.

Our traveling days are exciting, but I'm homesick for American food and conveniences, Abbie wrote in her diary. *Connecting with other Americans like the sweet down-to-earth Davidsons is something I will never forget.*

Grass Mountain was about 30 minutes outside of downtown Taipei. Abbie wrote:

> We take a taxi from the hotel, directing the driver in Mandarin. They drive so crazy that I pray we will get there in one piece. The streets are teeming with pedestrians, speeding cars, pedi-cabs, and cows. You can see the tiny houseboats with household supplies situated along the swampy riverbanks.

Abbie learned that the island was only a short distance from mainland China, and the rebels from the mainland were in the throes of economic expansion. Factories were producing textiles, apparel, and inexpensive footwear for American export. Americans were not yet allowed to travel to mainland China.

Abbie and Sam led two lives. One was in Asia. The other was in New York City, where her life was busy, taking the kids to Central Park and strolling the West Side avenues. Day to day, Sam was a demanding and mercurial man.

"My shoes need to be shined. Why didn't you get them shined?" Sam yelled. "Did my mother call?"

Her husband was always preoccupied with business and his parents.

"Marriage is not what I dreamed," she told her friend Roz. "Sam's business comes first, and then his family. The babies and I come last."

Abbie played the role of happy homemaker, keeping the apartment in excellent order and serving dinner on time for Sam's arrival, guessing what time that would be.

"Always have dinner ready when he comes in the door," Sophia told her. "Sam has to eat on time."

Sam had also told her straight out that her role was to be the charming, beautiful wife.

"I want you to be like Loretta Young. She wears feminine chiffon dresses and when she comes into the room, she is smiling and brimming with happiness."

I think I'm in trouble.

Chapter Twenty-Four

When Eve was an infant, only months old, Abbie was overwhelmed by her sweet, but cranky temperament. She was delicate and sometimes cried all night.

"She has an immature nervous system," said Dr. Gribetz, the pediatrician. Her in-laws were surprised by a baby with blonde hair and blue eyes.

"My dad was a blonde and my sister a redhead," said Abbie. "Look, her head is shaped like Sam's."

Manny nodded, "Yes, you are right."

She was such a pretty baby but restless and difficult. Excessive crying sometimes made Sam lose his temper.

"I'll give you something to cry about," he yelled.

Eve was about seven months old when Sam slapped her across her delicate face for the first time.

"What are you doing?" Abbie shouted. She picked up the baby and hugged her close, rubbing her little back. "Are you out of your mind? Don't ever do that again."

"She has to learn not to cry. I don't want a spoiled little screaming brat."

When Abbie told her mother-in-law about the incident, she was upset and assured her she would talk to her Samuel about it.

Bessie, Abbie's mother, was aggravated and gave her the old "I told you so." Abbie was becoming afraid of Sam, who was not the same sweet man who had written the love letters to her.

"Tell him to stop it," Bessie told Abbie. "He's a bully. I see how you walk on eggshells around him."

The dark side of their storybook marriage was unfolding. To make matters worse, Sam was out of town more and more and less communicative than ever, acting tense and solemn much of the time at home.

"I might have to make another trip to get the samples ready," Sam said. "I'm still coughing from being there so long the last trip."

He had developed a chronic respiratory condition. The doctor said, "It's from the climate there. It's sub-tropical. We used to call it Yokohama syndrome."

The baby slips happened when Sam was irritable. Abbie rationalized the behavior by thinking that maybe this kind of discipline would work. Maybe Sam was right. Her own methods of distracting Eve did not work. When she tried to amuse her with play and activities, she often continued her whining and crying.

Carol, Abbie's friend, noticed how hypersensitive Eve was to her surroundings.

"Look, I tiptoed into the room, and she shot up in her crib," Carol said. Abbie thought, "It true, when she naps, she wakes up at the sound of a breath or a tissue dropping."

Abbie played peek-a-boo with her pretty baby and walked her up and down Columbus Avenue and Central Park West. She engaged her in Sesame Street, a new show on television, and with their young neighbors.

As she started to crawl, Eve's new-found mobility lessened her jumpiness. One of her favorite activities became exploring in the kitchen and taking out all the pots and pans from the cabinets.

Sam's business and the extended trips ruled their lives. To stay current with fashion trends, Sam needed to check European trends and he usually took Abbie to London, Italy and Spain. Though she loved the travel, she dreaded leaving her young baby. Grandma and Grandpa flew up from Florida to babysit, but when Eve was seven months old, Sam agreed that they would take her with them to Paris and Italy.

That's how it happened that Eve went to Europe on her own passport. Mother and daughter in a stroller wandered the streets, munching on local breads. One night in a hotel in Lugano, Eve was crying inconsolably in her crib and they were unable to leave for dinner. Sam screamed at the baby to stop and slapped her across her face. Abbie picked her up and rocked her, then Sam said, "Come on, let's go downstairs and eat. She will fall asleep."

After that incident, they called in a babysitter to stay with Eve in the evenings.

Abbie suffered with the memory of that night and couldn't shake the horror of it. Sam thought nothing of the abuse. One day when she was visiting her in-laws, Abbie approached Manny about Sam's rage.

"A few smacks are nothing compared to how we were tortured and starved in Siberia," he said.

At 64, working for his son now, Manny liked to wear expensive pima cotton shirts and Ralph Lauren neck ties. He drove a BMW.

Abbie saw how embittered Manny was by war-time trauma. She wasn't sure what went on in his head. He usually wore a big smile on his face.

One day when she complained about being lonely during Sam's long trips, he shamed her. "Look at the life you have, this apartment, a big car. Soon you will be living in a big house in a beautiful town."

He pounded his big fist into his chest. "You think we put our memories in a drawer somewhere? You see this shirt, this tie. There is nothing here, nothing but bitterness."

Sam grew up playing the role of protector of his family. As a toddler, he was taught to beg for food from strangers in the camps. Now that he had become a successful businessman, his priority was his immigrant family — his parents and his young sister.

"My son, Samuel, will be somebody," Sophia liked to say. "He is our hero, a star."

Was it fair for Abbie to judge them? She could not possibly understand the demons that lived in their souls. Now Sam's wife and children…who were they to Sam? As time went by, she didn't know how to please him. And there was something of a mystery going on in the bedroom.

Positions she wasn't sure about… had never known about. She was afraid to ask her friends, maybe her mother … After all, her parents had kept Vaseline on their nightstand.

Other idiosyncrasies arose. One day, Sam started a to-do session in the living room and explained that he wanted to build a library of classic books, insisting that Abbie do extensive research to determine what the library should contain.

"I would like you to prepare a list of books we should buy," he said.

"I already can suggest to you what classic books to buy," she said. "Shakespeare, Hemingway, Tolstoy…" He scowled.

"I simply asked you to do some research and already you are giving me a hard time. Don't tell me you know about the books that belong in a library."

Another time, Sam wanted to learn about vitamins. "Abbie, I want you to read up on vitamins and report back to me about which ones we should be taking. Find out their benefits, and how the different vitamins work in our bodies."

Abbie studied some books and reported back to him about Vitamins C, K, and D. Her own doctor said too many vitamins could be harmful.

Over the next few years, Sam gradually began to follow a strict organic path…before organic became a household word. He was always ahead of the curve. Yes, he was a visionary in some ways, but he tended to go overboard. The traditional vitamin search, when Sam began to take Vitamin C, was the start of a regimen that became extreme. He moved far beyond the mainstream of traditional wellness, eventually falling into a worldwide network of holistic medicine healers — and dealers, some earnest, but many were con artists selling magic cures.

Chapter Twenty-Five

It happened during the trip to Italy. Another pregnancy.

"Eve, you are going to have a sister or brother," Abbie said.

"Yay," Eve said. She clapped her hands.

Abbie had a smooth pregnancy and decided to see a new obstetrician. Her friend, Carol, recommended Dr. Silverstein who delivered her son.

"I want a doctor who takes me seriously when I say I want natural childbirth," she told her friend Carol. "The doctor who delivered Eve gave me too much Pitocin and I had to be anesthetized during the delivery."

"Dr. Silverstein won't do that," Carol said. "He's very gentle and understanding."

The week of Abbie's due date, Sam had to leave for Topeka on a sales trip. Abbie begged him to reschedule the trip.

"I think I'm about to go into labor. I feel the baby's head pushing down. Please don't go."

"The baby can wait another week," Sam said as he headed out the door with his briefcase and overnight bag. "I'll only be away for one night."

Abbie was so certain of imminent labor that she decided to sleep at Carol's apartment, which was a few blocks from the hospital. Her mother-in-law stayed with Eve for the night. At 3 o'clock in the morning, Abbie went into labor and called Dr. Silverstein.

"My contractions are every 20 minutes," she was counting. Carol took her to the hospital.

When the doctor walked in and saw Carol in the delivery area, he said, "What are you doing here?"

When he examined Abbie, he confirmed, "You are five centimeters dilated." Halfway there.

"You are built to have babies," Dr. Silverstein said.

Abbie was groggy but awake when she gave birth to Lila, who weighed 9 pounds, two ounces. The beautiful baby had dark blue eyes and bronzed skin. When the nurse wheeled her into Abbie's room, the new mother in the next bed remarked, "That is the most beautiful baby I have ever seen."

Abbie called Sam in Kansas.

"You have another daughter. She is gorgeous. When are you coming home?"

"There is a snowstorm and the airport is shut down. I'm sorry, honey."

To his credit, Sam caught the first flight home the next day. The following week, Kansas was on the agenda; Sam took Abbie with him for a big steak dinner with the customers in Topeka.

Owners of a footwear chain in the Midwest, they toasted Abbie and Sam at the most popular chop house in town.

"Congratulations," they shouted. They placed a big order for women's sandals and slippers.

Their family seemed complete with two beautiful daughters, one bouncy petite blonde, and one calm and passive brunette. Abbie savored being a full-time mom with a twin-stroller. She took the girls to Central Park, morning and afternoon, where Eve played in the sand box while Lila slept in the carriage. She set up play dates with neighbors in the building, attended lots of family gatherings, and entertained visitors from out of town.

Sam took Abbie on two business trips a year to London, Paris and Italy to scout out fashion trends. At home, Abbie busied herself with decorating the apartment and hired a Park Avenue designer. She had come a long way from shopping at Goodwill and the Salvation Army.

"Your apartment should look like the palace at Versailles," said Edith Rose, the Park Avenue decorator. "We'll install antique white doors with gold trim to cover the windows, no draperies. It will be gorgeous."

Abbie couldn't picture what she was talking about, but the sliding doors turned out to be stunning, enhancing the entire living room and dining area. Much better than the fringed window shades she knew as a child or the dusty windows in the apartment with her roommates.

In only two years, her life had changed dramatically. They lived in a charming building on a main crosstown street on the burgeoning Upper West Side, where cafes and boutiques were popping up all along Columbus Avenue. Abbie's circle of friends grew as mommy groups met almost every afternoon of the week. They usually met in someone's apartment where they sipped wine and chatted about their children and husbands.

"My husband is opening another office," said one woman. "He's exhausted when he comes home."

"Mine is always playing golf on the weekends," someone else said. "We don't have enough family together time."

So, I'm not the only way with problems.

"Sam has to go on another trip," Abbie said. "It's really hard for me to be alone with the babies."

Lila would sit quietly in her infant seat and look all around. Abbie felt truly blessed she had friends and a successful husband. She also had close family nearby. That meant a lot to her.

Abbie spoke to her mother-in-law almost every day. Bessie, her own mother in Florida now, worried for Abbie. Things seemed to be too good to be true.

"He travels so much," said Bessie. "I don't trust him. What's he doing over there for weeks at a time? Men can't be without women for that long."

"Stop it, Mother. You always think the worst about everyone. I'm not worried. Sam is very loving to me."

All their friends would tell her that Sam was crazy about her. And the children, too, except for the occasional slaps.

Occasionally, Abbie daydreamed about Marty, the man she stayed in New York for, and wondered what had become of him. She also realized that happy times could turn sour. And that family loyalty could be fleeting. Her sister-in-law was getting a divorce after only a year of marriage to her long-time boyfriend.

Sam was away on a trip and Abbie took the babies to Chicago to visit her sister in Skokie. One freezing cold morning, she got an unexpected call from her father-in-law. Choked up in a shaky voice, Manny said that Rachel wanted a divorce from Mike.

"What happened?" Abbie asked in disbelief.

"He…he doesn't want to be with her. He doesn't want to sleep with her."

"I'm shocked. They were dating for so many years. What will happen to the condo in Brooklyn? What does Marie think?" She was Mike's elderly mother, a shy widow who made such a fuss over Rachel.

Soon Abbie noticed that pictures of Marie and Mike disappeared from the family albums. Someone cut up all the wedding pictures and as life went on, no mention of Rachel's marriage was ever made. It was as if the marriage had never happened.

Except for Abbie. She was the family photo keeper and she kept some photos of the bride and groom that had been taken at their extravagant wedding. With Sam's help, Rachel soon moved into the city. Her apartment got fully furnished and decorated by a professional designer. Rachel worked in the business with Sam and managed the office, now on Fifth Avenue near Grand Central Terminal.

The more Sam worked and left on trips, the more Abbie was lonely and thought about Marty. She thought about her early days in New York, and even told Sam about Marty.

Years later, she told her therapist, "It was a mistake telling my husband about my past adventures. It was immature of me. Naturally, he was jealous.

"If my first mistake was talking about an old boyfriend to Sam, then my second critical mistake was nagging him about being away from home so much. Successful men and women make sacrifices and feel their families have to do the same. I should have realized this long ago."

Her therapist said, "When you got married at 23 years old, you didn't know any better. You had no role models.

Your only reference point was your own family — your mother and father and older sister, but they were dysfunctional in many ways."

"I never thought of them that way. My dad came home every night after a hard day's work and had dinner. Then he fell asleep in a wingchair in front of the TV. My mother was talking on the phone or out playing cards."

Life in the 1950s was about playing outside and watching the new TV set. When she was five years old, Abbie played hopscotch in front of the building where she lived on a big boulevard across from a park. She had metal roller skates with a key and skated up and down the street, often by herself. Neighbors could keep an eye out. At night, everyone sat outside on folding chairs and chatted, while the kids caught fireflies in glass jars.

Sometimes, Abbie saw an elderly blind man walking home from the YMCA. She took his hand and walked with him. She made princess crowns out of shirt cardboards and tin foil. She didn't go to pre-school or play groups. In kindergarten, which she started when she was nearly six years old, she learned how to hang up her coat in the cloak room and play songs on the xylophone and metal triangle. When she was 11 years old, she started to babysit, earning 50 cents an hour. The family she worked for taught her how to take care of their infant and two children.

No one had ever really hit Abbie. Except when she was a teenager and spoke back to her mother, who would chase her around the dining room table and swat her with a kitchen towel. She didn't get a lot of attention and lived internally, worrying about issues with friends and school, and daydreaming about a life of love and romance. She imagined herself teaching the deaf or blind, changing the world.

Now Abbie lived in a big city with a husband whose family had survived the Holocaust. She complained to her husband that he traveled too much. He usually didn't answer. He was distant, even silent, and rough in the bedroom. He wanted to be a magnate and she didn't really know for sure what she wanted from life. She knew she wanted to be a good mother. That much she knew.

Yes, Sam wanted to be successful and wealthy, something Abbie was not yet able to grasp. After all, her childhood role models were Donna Reed and Debbie Reynolds. Back then, the Kardashians did not exist.

Chapter Twenty-Six
Winter 1971

One evening in the winter of 1971, as Abbie was bringing dessert to the dinner table, Sam started to talk about getting a larger apartment.

"I think we're ready for a larger place, maybe a co-op in the city. Maybe even a house in the suburbs," he said. "I have made enough money to move up."

Abbie had no idea how much money they had but she did notice how much they spent on furnishings and how often they went out to fancy restaurants and entertained business associates from out of town. They had a steady housekeeper, too.

"How much do we have to buy an apartment? Or a house?"

Eve was three years old and Lila was 18 months. "I agree that we need more space, and room enough for one more child."

In the back of her mind, she wanted to give him a son.

Abbie was ambivalent about moving to the suburbs, especially to Westchester County, known for exclusive country clubs where golf was the main activity. It felt too rich for her taste. She was used to walking on city streets, taking taxis and buses, and socializing in Central Park playgrounds.

She loved the diversity of urban life, the noise, and the ethnic restaurants. She enjoyed taking the subway and seeing faces from every national background, discovering parks, diners, and restaurants in every corner of the city, uptown and downtown. New York was a cornucopia of culture and cuisine.

They agreed to start looking. "We can start by looking in Manhattan and then maybe look in the suburbs," Sam said.

Sam used his connections to find a real estate broker who knew of a beautiful duplex apartment on Park Avenue. That Saturday, they went to see it. The owner was the widow of a famous CEO on Wall Street. She was getting remarried to a real estate tycoon who had a grander apartment on Central Park West.

Abbie and Sam wandered through the spacious apartment.

"This is amazing. I love the living room and dining room. The kitchen is perfect," Abbie said. "I love white cabinets and the marble floors are incredible."

"Very nice," Sam said. "Let's look upstairs."

They were disappointed. "The master bedroom is elegant," Abbie said. "But there is only one other bedroom for two children to share."

"This will never work for our family," Sam scowled. "Let's go."

Frustrated, they agreed to go house hunting in Northern New Jersey. Neither of them knew anything about the area. One Saturday, a broker took them to look at small mansions in Englewood Cliffs and colonial-style houses in Tenafly.

The broker mentioned all the famous people who lived there. "One drawback is that some of the public schools are not that good," she said. "You might have to send your kids to private school."

"We're not sure where to look," Abbie told her friends watching their kids play in the park. "We looked at a few towns in New Jersey, but really we don't know anyone there. Sam dislikes the commute to Grand Central."

"You should look in Westchester County, there are some great school districts," said Leslie, whose daughter went to nursery school with Eve. "You can get more space and there are good public schools."

Their search started again in several Westchester towns. They had heard about Harrison and Pleasantville. A white-haired lady from a top real estate sales office took them for a tour of gorgeous properties. She even took them to Chappaqua and Scarsdale, two of the most expensive areas.

"Sam, this is overwhelming. Should we really be moving up here?"

He acted unfazed by the prices and size of the properties.

"We can handle this. I mostly am interested in the commuter time it will take me to get to Grand Central Terminal," Sam said.

Abbie agreed with that sentiment. "Absolutely, you don't want to spend hours on a train."

Abbie was awed by the expansive colonial style houses on big lots with lush landscapes. She couldn't believe how grand they were, so comfortable and roomy.

"We are going to need a lot of furniture," she said.

Mrs. Fitzgerald, the white-haired lady from the sales office, said. "You would love it up here. I can help you find a decorator."

One real estate agent had them looking at homes way over their budget of $100,000. That seems like an awful lot of money, thought Abbie.

Another Saturday, they went looking more seriously in Pleasantville, an established community on the Peekskill commuter railroad line where people seemed low-keyed and less showy than some of the other communities. It was affluent, yet quaint at the same time. The houses were smaller and older, with a neighborly feel. The train line went directly into Grand Central, a block from Sam's office.

Then Sam saw a house he loved. It was a sprawling Colonial-style house with five bedrooms and three-and-a-half bathrooms on an acre of land in the choicest section of Pleasantville village. There were two bonus rooms on a third-floor level that was probably intended for the help.

The house smelled of chocolate chip cookies baking in the oven. It was immaculate, beautiful at first glance. There was a circular driveway and a slate roof.

"It's a lovely house," she said. "But isn't it too big for us?"

Sam loved it. It was $160,000. He had decided.

A few days before Sam was going to sign the contract, Abbie had a premonition. Perhaps it was because she felt a sore throat coming on, but she had a feeling that it was a wrong move. She couldn't explain why. The house was spacious and traditional, not at all ostentatious, but it was not what she would consider a cozy place to live.

Sam's father had other ideas. He thought it was perfect for his successful son.

To Abbie, the house was not modern enough, too expensive, and she did not know a single person in a 30-mile radius. But it wasn't her decision to make, really. The family dictated their future.

At Eve's third birthday, Manny said, "I see you living in a big house with a big driveway…this is what you want," Manny said, sweeping his arm in a grand gesture.

A few weeks later, the family packed up and moved out of Manhattan, where Abbie had lived since the time she had moved from Chicago. Many of their friends in the city soon followed, because they needed more space and free public schools. A few families moved to New Jersey. Leslie and her husband and kids moved to White Plains. Pleasantville turned out to be a beautiful town with friendly people. Abbie's best friend, Carol, followed them to Pleasantville less than a year later.

Abbie enrolled Eve in a nursery school. At the town recreation center, she signed up for tennis lessons.

In a new tennis white dress she had bought at the Tennis Lady boutique, she forced herself to register for classes twice a week.

A nice lady gave her a schedule of classes and registered her for two mornings a week of tennis lessons.

"I signed up for advanced beginner tennis classes," Abbie told Sam.

"You sure look good in that white outfit," Sam said. "I love the panties."

He was not interested in golf or country clubs, so it became her job to make friends and entertain. And they were able to afford live-in help, an Irish woman, and later a wonderful woman named Ginger from Barbados, who stayed with them for four years.

Abbie's old hang-ups made her uncomfortable about entertaining. She had been afraid to even host a club meeting in the apartment where she grew up. She pushed herself to host dinner parties and luncheons, showing off her extravagant crystal and china. Her childhood issues with messy bedrooms and disheveled linen closets subsided. Now she had help and the means to fashion an orderly household.

One morning, Abbie was talking to a friend on the phone. "Sam is away again. I've got two kids in a gigantic house in the suburbs. My husband is constantly away."

There were longer and longer stays in the Far East checking on shoe samples, negotiating deals. Except for the housekeeper who lived in for five days of the week, she was alone with her two darling daughters.

Sam would call Abbie and the kids once a week. He was in touch with his office daily via a telex machine. Orders would electronically go back and forth.

Abbie kept busy, but the isolation was wearing on her nerves.

One Sunday, her in-laws came over for lunch. She complained to Sophia, her mother-in-law, about being lonely.

"This is the way it is," Sophia said. "I understand, but Sam wants to be somebody. You have to be a good wife."

Abbie's mother in Chicago was more sympathetic. "You're all alone there. It's not what you expected."

Bessie did not fail to remind her of the possibilities of marital infidelity and deception.

"Who knows what he's doing over there. Men will be men."

Chapter Twenty-Seven

In 1974, Sam had extensive business in Hong Kong for two weeks.

"I want you to come with me on this trip," Sam said. "Your parents can stay with the girls and Ginger."

"I don't want to travel so far away from the girls," Abbie told her friend Carol. "Leaving them for two weeks gives me such anxiety."

Abbie had just turned 30 years old and she felt the weight of this milestone. She thought about flying on so many trips.

My number might be up. Maybe we only get a certain number of safe flights.

At night she couldn't stop herself from having harrowing thoughts of dying in a plane crash. Feelings of panic overwhelmed her.

The flight to Taipei, with a stopover in Anchorage, Alaska, took about 21 hours. Usually, they stopped in Tokyo for a couple of nights to meet with business partners. From Taipei to Hong Kong, was about two or three hours.

They had to be in the air for 10 hours or more at a time to get to Anchorage. Then it was on to the Far East. Abbie became obsessed with being separated from her children. Fear consumed her.

"I'm afraid to go," she told Sam. "What if something happens to us? Our children won't have any parents."

Sam became irritated and angry.

"You are making me afraid to travel, and I have to go because it's my business. You can stay home, but I have to make these trips. If you don't want to come, maybe it's better you stay home."

Abbie was afraid that would ruin her marriage.

Faced with imagined disaster, exaggerated or not, Abbie didn't know who to turn to, who to ask for reassurance. She couldn't ask her mother because her mother would predict a catastrophe.

On the Saturday before the trip, Sam was finishing up at his office. Abbie left the children at home with the housekeeper and took the train into Manhattan. She headed for B. Altman department store on 34th Street and Fifth Avenue. She wandered around aimlessly, sick to her stomach, and found the women's room where there was an entire room full of black rotary pay phones and telephone booths with doors that closed for privacy. Thick phone books from every state in the country were on elevated tables for researching call numbers.

What should I do? Should I go, should I stay? My husband will leave me, hate me if I don't go. But if I die, the children will grow up without a mother.

Abbie couldn't control her thoughts. She was in a state of panic.

She looked through the New York City telephone book and found the Yellow Pages. Browsing through names of psychics who lived on the Upper East side. Trembling, Abbie picked up the clumsy black phone in one of the booths, and called Julia, clairvoyant and astrologist, who was located in the neighborhood.

"Good morning," said a woman in a gentle, smooth voice.

"Good morning," replied Abbie. "I have an odd situation and need help in making a crucial decision." She explained the upcoming trip and her fear of flying and leaving her young children.

"Would you like to come by. I have time to see you today."

"Yes, please. I can be there in a half hour."

Out on the corner of 34th and Madison Avenue, Abbie hailed a taxi and told the driver to take her to the corner of 59th and Third Avenue. When they got there, the reddish-brick doorman building looked familiar. She had passed it many times.

The doorman announced her arrival and she stepped into the elevator, feeling ridiculous. But when Julia answered the door, she was relieved to see a kind-looking, elderly woman in a cotton housedress and slippers. She had gentle gray eyes and thinning white hair caught in a bun.

"Hello, please come in, I'm Julia." She took Abbie's hand and led her into the living room. "Would you like a glass of water?" she asked.

"I would like some water, thank you," said Abbie. "You must think I'm crazy to be in such a frantic state of mind."

"No, not at all. This is what I do. I help people make decisions about their future. Tell me your concerns and why you are going on this trip."

Abbie explained and emphasized her fear of flying so far away from her children.

Then Julia asked her, "What is your birth date? Do you know what time you were born and where?"

Abbie told her. Then Julia went into her small office and worked for about 20 minutes. Abbie fidgeted anxiously on the couch, listening to the city street noises.

Finally, Julia came and sat down on a nearby chair, close to Abbie. "Your chart looks good. You don't have to worry about this trip. You will be safe," said Julia, radiating immense certainty.

"Nothing will happen to you on this trip to Asia. But you may have some problems in the next few years. You will be able to deal with your fate, and what I see is that you very much want to be somebody. And this is interesting, too. When you are 80 years old, you will look more like 40," she said. "My dear, enjoy the trip and pay attention to your husband. He is very ambitious. More than you know."

Abbie thanked her and told her how relieved she was.

"Are you sure?"

"Yes, I'm sure."

The next day, they were all packed and ready to go to the airport.

"The girls will be fine," said Abbie's mother.

Abbie and Sam kissed their darling children good-bye. Her heart was heavy, though she tried to hide her fears from her husband. She clung to Julia's prediction, but she kept thinking about the airplane and doubted that it could lift off.

How will the plane get over the mountain she remembered seeing in Hong Kong harbor?

Abbie was careful not to lay her fears on Sam again. Once they arrived in Hong Kong, that magnificent, exotic city on a harbor, Sam got busy with work. Abbie was free to roam around and shop, but she spent a lot of time in their luxurious room at the Mandarin Hotel. There was a big window she could see from their king-size bed. She stared out the window, thinking about how the plane would lift off and get them back home. At times, she felt immovable, agonizing about getting airborne. It seemed impossible.

One afternoon, Sam took her shopping for a jade ring, the one she was supposed to have gotten as an engagement ring. They looked at many beautiful rings, but Abbie couldn't make a decision.

One night at dinner, Sam said, "You don't seem like your usual cheerful self."

"I'm OK, just miss the kids," she said.

The trip was uneventful, like Julia promised. The gods did not strike and once their homeward bound plane touched down, Abbie was elated. The anxiety and depression lifted, and she knew she wanted to give life to one more child. She wanted so much to please Sam and secure their marriage.

In mid-June of 1974, they planned to try for another baby, following a current method that promised to increase the odds for the gender of your choice. It involved creating an acidic or alkaline solution in your vagina.

On June 14, a Friday, Sam and Abbie went to bed early and set to work. About two weeks later, Abbie was overcome by a hot flash. She knew her hormones had kicked in and a baby was beginning.

"You're right," said Dr. Silverstein. "You are pregnant."

The first months of the pregnancy went smoothly. Abbie felt calmer than she had for a long time, except she started to feel a more pronounced disconnect with Sam.

One night, he called up and said, "I will be a little late getting home. A rep is in town and, uh, I have to take him out to dinner."

Sam's voice sounded shaky, like he was trembling. More evenings like that followed, and Abbie wondered. By September, when she was in her fourth month, she started to show. The distance between her and Sam seemed to grow proportionately with the size of her belly.

When Sam came home, usually at about 7 p.m., he was quieter than usual, a bit glum. He was less interested in what she had prepared for dinner. He stopped kissing her except when they had sex, which was occasional. As the months went by and autumn turned to winter, Sam wasn't home much. He took short trips and when he was around, he nagged her about having the baby on time.

Sam had already made two trips to Japan during the summer but then toward the end of the year, he said, "Listen, I don't know what your plans are, but I have to go to Tokyo again and I can't put it off much longer."

"In case you haven't noticed, I'm in my seventh month. My due date is March 6, what do you want me to do?" Abbie sounded weak, defeated.

Since that snowy anniversary night at Lutèce, when he had practically stood her up at the Regency Hotel, he was even more distant.

Their bed felt icy. Abbie sensed her heart shriveling. She tried to hold on to hope that things might get better after the baby was born. Especially if she had a son. The unthinkable was in the back of her mind. *Maybe he has a girlfriend. Or maybe he is just sick of me being pregnant.*

One day in late December, near Christmas, Abbie went into New York with her friend Jenny Priestley, a Brit, and Jen's mother-in-law, who was visiting from London. Loretta Priestley was a tall, sophisticated woman with lovely auburn hair and amber eyes.

Abbie sat next to her on the crowded commuter train and confided in her about her martial problems. Abbie told her how Sam had become passionless and distant. He was hard and unaffectionate. She recounted their last trip to Hong Kong and his subsequent trips to Japan without her.

Loretta lowered her head and whispered softly in Abbie's ear. "It doesn't sound good. I think what you are feeling in your heart is real," she said in her clipped British accent. "Your husband might have another interest, I'm sorry to say. Wait and see what happens, and you will soon know what you must do."

Abbie was almost seven months pregnant! That same day, as they walked up Fifth Avenue amid bright Christmas decorations and tinkling Salvation Army bells, they ran into Sam walking hurriedly by his office building. He stopped to say hello, as a stranger would. Stiffly, he let Abbie know that his company was holding a Christmas party. And that he would be home late. Abbie had no previous knowledge of this.

Abbie gripped her somersaulting stomach. Her head was going to burst with pain.

"My poor baby," she thought. *My poor baby is not going to have a father.*

Chapter Twenty-Eight

Years later, Abbie would vividly remember the time her marriage began to unravel and crash. The devastation…the sudden shock when she was in her seventh month.

Of course, her mother had warned her. Sam denied that there were other women. He wasn't cheating on her.

Abbie thought to herself. Maybe my mother is right. He might have met an exotic Asian woman on a plane or at a hotel bar.

Abbie, let's not get ahead of the story.

During those miserable days in late December 1974, Abbie's heart was shattering in pieces and her mind was filled with dread and fear for the well-being of her innocent unborn baby tucked away in her expanding uterus. She couldn't remember any other time in her life when things had seemed so hopeless and uncertain. The days dragged on in an unbearable state of limbo.

If only I could hurry this up to see what happens. If I could only do something about it.

Each night, Sam came home late and was glacial. Solemn as a devout evangelist. But he always ate the dinner she had ready.

Later, once the divorce case commenced, and he was still in the house, Sam stopped eating the food in the kitchen. He glared at her and pointedly said, "I think you might poison me."

It happened a day or two after one of the legal motions during the summer after she gave birth, after he alleged that she was an unfit mother.

It must have been in July or August after the baby was born. By that time, she intensely wished he would move out, but his lawyer advised him to remain in the house. He came home and went into the kitchen. Still in his business suit and one of his blue shirts, with the sleeves rolled up, he eyed the crusty brown pot roast and potatoes and put his nose in the pot to smell it. Then he walked away and took a glass of milk.

During the final two months of her pregnancy, Abbie held on to shreds of hope that Sam's attitude would miraculously pass. He came home late, but he returned every night and they still shared the same bed. Despite her despair, the children were a distraction, and she was learning to play bridge to distract her fearful thoughts.

She confided in no one, except her nervous mother. "I'm learning bridge and doing some needlepoint," she told Bessie. "I have to get through the days and nights until the baby comes. Until I can figure this all out."

None of her friends knew there was trouble at home. She complained to Carol about Sam's traveling and prolonged periods out of the country, but that was nothing new. She didn't dare say that he was planning to divorce her.

The evening before her bridge club in early January, she expected Sam to come home for dinner. She waited for him and Eve and Lila listened for the garage door to open.

"Is Daddy coming home soon?" asked Eve, now five years old.

It grew late and the girls went to bed. Hour by hour, a sickening feeling grew in Abbie's belly. She called Sam's office repeatedly, but the phone just kept ringing. She heard his threatening words in her brain, "I'm tired of doing everything that other people want. I want to take care of myself for a change and do what makes me happy."

Then she started to think clearly. *It's always about you and the war and your family. It's about settling in America and making money. Your parents and sister always come first. Never mind about me, our marriage, our children. Why did you want to have another baby? I know: you want a son. We planned this pregnancy together. I got pregnant the first night we tried.*

Her brain spun in circles. She tossed and turned all night and did not sleep for a minute. Sleep was impossible. By the time morning came, she was exhausted and spent. Her bloated body ached with wretchedness and pregnancy hormones. Then at 7:30 a.m., the phone rang, breaking the numbing silence in the house.

"Hi, it's Sam. How are you doing?" Then too quickly, "I'm sorry I couldn't get home last night. There was something I had to do."

"Where were you? Why didn't you call?" Just silence. He was the only person she ever knew who didn't answer questions. He negotiated that way in business. At that point, he ended the conversation, saying ever so softly, "I hope you have a lovely day." Then he hung up.

Abbie fell to the floor and cried and cried. She thought she would die, but she knew she couldn't abandon her two little daughters and a baby was in her stomach..."my poor, poor baby," she wretchedly moaned.

She faced herself in the mirror. *"There is nothing you can do about this until you have the baby. Please, God, give me strength."*

She could barely move to get dressed for bridge. The thought of going to Jennifer's to play a game of cards made her nauseous. She didn't want to see her friends or talk to anyone. But she looked forward to drowning her mind in the cards, in the bridge hands, getting lost in the strategy, putting her anxious body out of misery.

Carol picked her up at 11 am. "You look so pale," she remarked. "What's wrong?" Abbie realized she had not applied any make-up.

The two women arrived at Jennifer's house, an old Tudor with rainbow-glass windows, and Abbie spied a crowd of women inside, all dressed up and smiling. As she and Carol entered, they all yelled "Surprise!" with great fervor. Her heart plummeted.

Abbie's mother-in-law and sister-in-law were there. It was a surprise baby shower. She was struck dumb by the joyful shouts.

She let out a cry of shock and dismay. She collapsed in tears of sorrow.

"What's wrong? What's the matter with you?" one of her friends asked. "What are you crying about?"

Her close friend Davida tried to comfort her. She said, "Is there something wrong? Is the baby OK?"

Carol took her into the bathroom. Finally, Abbie whispered. "I haven't told you. Sam wants to leave me."

In a flash, Abbie thought about Sam's early morning call. *He must have known about the shower and called to wish me a lovely day.*

Carol gasped. "Oh, my God." Finally, Carol gently took hold of her arm and led her from the bathroom. The others huddled in shock, whispering to one another. No one knew what to say or do. Everyone dispersed without an explanation.

Abbie's mother-in-law Sophia came to her side and put her arms around her. She knew something but didn't say a word. They spoke every day on the phone. She let her babysit for short periods, even though she could barely handle the diapers.

Abbie was sure Sophia was wondering why she didn't work things out with Sam. That thought made her look totally depleted, and she just wanted to go home and crawl under the covers and never come out again. Finally, Carol led her out of the house. What was it her mother-in-law always used to say? About the holocaust. About tough times and suffering.

"Life is a dream," Sophia always said. "Sometimes it's good and sometimes it's a horror. It's a tragedy."

Today had been a bad, bad dream. Later, she made dinner for the kids finding comfort in her own kitchen away from the hurtful world.

I will push through an ocean of depression to be a good mother.

Then the phone rang. It was Brigitte Miller, one of the bridge players from the party. She was a heavy-set, matronly woman who spoke pretentiously and bragged about her stockbroker husband and little son. She barely knew Abbie, except through bridge.

"Hello, Abbie," the woman said, her voice gruff. "I just had to tell you this one thing. You're a terrible person. We all went out of our way to set up a beautiful shower for you, and you acted like a monster. I have never seen anyone behave like that."

Abbie drew a jagged breath. She felt demolished, horribly devastated to the core of her being. She couldn't do anything right. She plowed through the next weeks in a blurry haze of despair, utterly terrified by what was happening to her ordered life and her children's lives. She worried about the baby's well-being *in utero*, but the precious one was strong.

Chapter Twenty-Nine
March 1975

Abbie gave birth to her beautiful daughter, Sara, on March 4, 1975. Oddly, a couple of weeks before her due date, Sam cancelled his trips and stayed close to home. They even played bridge with Carol and her husband when Abbie went into labor close to 9 p.m. Sam drove her to the hospital in the city and was by her side. Dr. Silverstein arrived about 10:30, and at 1 a.m., Sara emerged into the world through natural childbirth. Finally, no drugs at all.

Sara had her father's coloring. You could see that right away. She had dark hair on her round head, and a lean body. The doctor told the attending nurse, "Give her the baby."

Abbie held her whole and perfect child. "You made it, we made it," she murmured to her baby. Then, for precautionary reasons, the doctor had the infant placed in the neonatal unit for one day's observation. He said there had been stressful circumstances surrounding her gestation and he wanted to make sure she was completely healthy.

Abbie snuck up to the neonatal floor every few hours to see if Sara was okay in her antiseptic bubble. Once, she saw the interns making their rounds and heard them say to each other, "What's wrong with this baby?" She weighed exactly eight pounds and was a perfect infant with thick dark hair and long spindly legs.

Abbie giggled to herself. "We are going to be fine. Everything is going to be copacetic."

Sara looked more like her sister Lila than blonde, fair-haired Eve, who was petite and active as a tiny acrobat. Eve showed signs of a penchant for cooking, always getting into the kitchen cupboards and drawers, and stirring the puddings and cake mix for her mother. She was still prone to moods, but affectionate and loving.

After Abbie brought the new daughter home from the hospital, she watched her sleeping in her crib that first night. Sam quietly came into the nursery, without a whisper. Abbie looked at him and asked, "Isn't she precious?"

"Yes, she's beautiful." He stared at the baby. But didn't look at Abbie.

"Can't we work things out? There must be a way to keep our family together. I'll do whatever you want," said Abbie.

He said no, he wanted to separate. "I'm tired of trying to make other people happy. I need to do something for myself now." Then he added the stinger. "Our marriage is already over, as far as I am concerned."

You are a mad man. How can you do this to me at this time in our lives?

"I'm still your wife and I will always be the mother of your children."

Sam looked at her for a moment, then spun on his heels and left the nursery.

Chapter Thirty
April 1975

Though he wanted a divorce, Sam refused to move out of the house. He slept in the children's playroom.

If that's what he wants, I'll give him a divorce.

The day that Sara was one month old, Abbie took the train into the city and walked up 53rd Street to Vincent Malone's office, the matrimonial lawyer that handled celebrity divorces. Malone had agreed to see her through a connection. Abbie had no idea what a divorce was about or what it cost. All she had was a weekly allowance of $278 and one municipal bond worth $5000.

As she ambled past corporate skyscrapers and townhouses, she steeled herself for a battle. Free from being pregnant with an innocent baby, she felt empowered. She was beautiful and thin. After the baby's birth, she went right back to her pre-Sara weight. The baby was thriving. She still lived in her beautiful house, had a live-in housekeeper, and a baby nurse hired for seven weeks.

I could try and stick out this marriage. Let him do what he wants. But it's not quite that simple.

She would not be a free woman. Sam would be waiting for her to make a wrong move, friends told her. He could follow her and go for custody. That's what her friends said. That's what she read in books about divorce.

She had to get a divorce. She was still young and could find another husband and father for her children. She had the feeling that this divorce thing was not going to be simple.

The office secretary introduced Abbie to Malone, a cordial older gentleman. He wore a light gray flannel suit, a starched white shirt, and a yellow bow tie. His dark blonde hair, edged with white, was parted on the side. A pipe rested on his desk alongside pictures of two teenage children who looked like their names might be Muffy and Buffy.

"How do you do," Malone said stiffly. "I'm sorry we have to meet this way."

"Me, too," said Abbie. "Can you help me?"

"Let's see. How do you know your husband wants a divorce? Does he have a lawyer?"

"Yes, he does. He told me several times and he behaves like he's in a hurry," He wrote me a note that says his lawyer is Ira Wexler."

"Let's make sure your husband is serious about this divorce." He picked up the phone and told his secretary to connect him with Sam's lawyer.

"Good morning, Ira. How are you?"

Abbie watched Malone nodding his head and holding his unlit pipe in his mouth.

"Thank you. I'm fine," replied Malone. "I have a young woman here named Abbie Cooperman."

"Uh-huh. Yes, that's right. Abbie tells me that her husband, Sam Cooperman, is pursuing a divorce and that you are representing him."

"Okay, yes. Then I can confirm that you are his attorney."

After a quick good-bye, Malone hung up with Wexler.

"You've got it right, young lady," Malone declared. "That is most unfortunate."

Without discussing a retainer fee or anything else, Malone instructed Abbie to go home as fast as possible and hide her valuables at a friend's house.

Thinking about what she had — a dozen antique Chinese porcelain pots and sterling silver flatware — Abbie felt panicked. Her mission was to run home and follow Malone's instructions.

On the train, Abbie was uncertain about Malone. She had forgotten to ask questions and everything was up in the air.

He's not the right lawyer for me. I need someone with empathy.

A few days later, her neighbor and friend, Michelle Crystal, whose husband was a corporate attorney, called Abbie.

"Malcolm met a brilliant lawyer in court today. His name is Daniel Benowitz," Michelle said. "You have to call him."

Chapter Thirty-One

Daniel Benowitz was a partner at Bartlett, Moore, and Benowitz, a boutique law firm in midtown Manhattan at 31st and Park. A week after she had seen Malone, Abbie went into the city again. She walked the short distance from Grand Central Terminal, breathing in the spring air and taking in the sights that she loved so much. This was no stroll in the park, she thought, as she moved briskly alongside suited men and women coming and going to their jobs.

I wonder if I will ever be one of these people going to work, engaging in a profession, making a living. Abbie knew that she would have to become more independent. Be a mother and a woman with a career.

In 1975, New York was a pulsating city of millions of workers on the move. Women found jobs mostly as administrative assistants and clerical workers. Many worked in the garment district, in advertising agencies and public relations firms. Some women had the foresight to enter finance and banking fields.

The only friend that Abbie knew who had gone into banking was her French-speaking roommate Yvonne, who had come home groaning every night about her miserable boss and the rigors of finance.

During the same time Abbie realized how dependent she was on a man, Diane von Furstenberg, a refugee from Austria, was making headlines in the garment industry.

She introduced the wrap dress, a style that was a sharp turn away from the prim shirtwaist dress or the corduroy jumper. In an era of pantyhose and pumps, it became wildly popular.

In the 1970s, married women and especially those with young children were mostly at home raising their kids. Most waited until their children reached junior high or high school before returning to the work force and starting over again with less status and lower wages than their male counterparts. It was tough to catch up with the latest information and the beginnings of technology, leaving women financially dependent on their husbands.

Women who were nurses often married doctors, only to give up their careers once they had children. Or they worked in their husbands' medical or dental practices, often performing administrative tasks. Without question, it was still a man's world.

Abbie's road to becoming a teacher was a back-up plan. *I never thought I would ever again have to support myself.*

Teaching was in case your husband got hit by a car or had a heart attack. Women talked about it all the time.

"If my husband dies, I can always go back to teaching," said Doreen, her roommate from college. "Or I can teach part-time to make extra money."

But now that Sam wanted a divorce, he expected Abbie to support herself and the children. She was supposed to pull a rabbit out of a hat. She had been reminded that their six-bedroom, three-bathroom house belonged to him, and the deed could not be transferred. He was the sole owner. He had always told her it was for insurance or tax purposes.

I was pretty stupid.

"It's not your fault," said Carol, her friend, who was pregnant again with her fourth child.

Abbie had been living in a cocoon, cushioned by the trappings of affluence. She was oblivious to the war raging in Viet Nam and the protest movement, unaware of the women's rights movement, clueless about money, investments, and life insurance. When Sam asked her to sign their joint tax return, she did not even look at it. She was busy finding the right nursery schools for her children, setting up afterschool events for them, and learning how to play tennis.

In her suburban splendor, Abbie lost track of the outside world. She was barely aware of the hippie movement until tidy little giggly Susan, one of her summer roommates during her break-up with Marty, came to visit, wearing a beaded Native American headband and a granny dress. Susan looked different with long, straight hair, except she was the same chatty airhead girl with dimples and a toothy smile.

It so happened that the day she went for her first meeting with Daniel Benowitz, Abbie wore her only Diane Von Furstenberg wrap dress. It was green and white and fit her perfectly, even though she had a five-week-old baby. She wore her Ferragamo bone patent leather pumps and a designer handbag with white and beige trim.

The reception area of the office was small and undecorated. Somewhat dark with no windows.

"I have an appointment with Mr. Benowitz," Abbie stated to the young woman at the oblong reception desk. "My name is Abbie Cooperman." Nervously, she shifted her handbag from one shoulder to the other. Soon a secretary emerged from a door next to the reception desk.

"Hi, I'm Janice. Dan is expecting you."

She led Abbie down a long hall to a small cluttered office with dingy blinds on the windows. She tentatively stepped into the space, scared and dreading the meeting.

Dan was sitting behind his desk with a black phone at his ear and a cigarette between his lips. Sit down, he said and motioned for her to take a seat.

She waited politely until he ended his call, eyeing the mountains of manila folders everywhere: on the brown wooden desk, behind the desk, on top of bookshelves, all over the floor.

He doesn't seem very organized, but he's a lot more informal than the other lawyer with the bowtie.

Abbie saw a college diploma on the wall. He had gone to Columbia University Law School.

Now he was nodding at her and smoking a cigarette.

"Speak to ya later," Benowitz hung up the phone.

"Don't mind the mess." He stood and shook Abbie's damp hand exuberantly. "By the way, please call me Dan."

His warm and confident smile eased her nerves. His crinkled light-blue button-down shirt was coming out of his waistband. They talked about Malcolm Crystal, their mutual contact, and how they knew him.

"The Crystals are my neighbors. Michelle Crystal is one of my only friends still talking to me," Abbie said.

"Really nice guy, good litigator. So, you're here about a divorce. I guess that's why your friends are giving you the cold shoulder. There are a lot of rifts when you divorce…for many reasons. People feel threatened…jealous and afraid. They think divorce is contagious."

"You know, I'm actually more of an entertainment lawyer, show business people and sports figures. It's all about negotiation. I take on some divorce cases when they interest me, especially if custody is an issue."

That was the first time Abbie thought about custody. *Do people actually fight each other for their children?*

Benowitz saw her glancing at his photos beside the heavy glass ash tray full of cigarette butts. "That's my wife, Joan, and my two daughters."

"So how long are you married?" he asked.

"Seven years, a little more."

"How many children do you have?"

"Three. One is an infant."

"The children are of tender age," he said.

His eyebrows lifted and he reached for a fresh cigarette. They were Parliaments.

"Do you know if your husband has a girlfriend?"

"No. I asked him that. He said, there's no other woman. He's just not happy. I guess we're not compatible.

"Maybe it's my fault. I nagged him too much about travelling. But I'm always lonely. Raising the children while he's away doing business."

Benowitz half-smiled. He was a tall, husky man, though not actually fat. He looked disheveled, as if he had forgotten to comb his hair, or maybe had slept overnight in his office. He had light brown hair, slightly streaked with blonde, and a prominent nose.

His eyes are pale blue, like Marty's eyes. Why am I thinking about Marty?

Sam had hazel eyes, beautiful eyes that could be so kind, and then terribly cruel. Once he kicked their Golden Retriever puppy all the way across the room.

I felt sick. That puppy ran away and we never saw the poor thing again.

"When did he tell you that he wanted a divorce? Were you surprised?"

"I was seven months pregnant. I was shocked."

Benowitz didn't look like a man who could be easily shaken. "What? In your seventh month?"

"Yes. That's right. He says he's not happy and he's tired of trying to make other people happy. I begged him to see a marriage counselor with me, but he wouldn't go. He's still living at home."

"Did you ask him to move out?"

"I did, yes, but he won't. It's his house. I mean the house is in his name. He moved into the playroom, comes and goes as he pleases. Some nights he doesn't come home at all."

Abbie told Benowitz that her parents had come to stay for a while. They lived in Florida now. Her father had retired but still worked a few days a week as an optician. Her mother wanted to stay with Abbie for a few more weeks, as long a time as is necessary.

"My parents are worried and upset," said Abbie. "My mom is a nervous woman."

Benowitz scribbled notes on a yellow legal pad. Then he precisely went over New York matrimonial law with her. In 1975, New York was a title state. "That means if your name is on a property, you own it,"

"Since your name is not on the deed to the house, you have no ownership rights. Unless Sam agrees to turn it over to you. Your name is on the title of your Mercedes Benz and on the title of your green Volkswagen hatchback. That means you are the owner. It's that simple."

In a divorce settlement, not even the court has the power to change the deed, without the legal consent of the title holder.

The house belonged solely to Sam, and he was responsible for paying the mortgage and the taxes. He had to make those payments, but as far as repairs or gardening, he could let the lawn go to rot.

"In a contractual agreement, Sam could transfer the house to you, if he chooses to. He could give you whatever he wants to. Some husbands are generous and give their wives and children large sums of money and property."

Theoretically, the woman was supposed to be supported in the style to which she had become accustomed, especially if it was a long marriage, but legally, everything had to be won through negotiation. There were precedents to follow, customary payouts, but at that time, there were no established formulas written in the state marital code. Abbie was not automatically entitled to anything, unless her name was on it.

"As your lawyer, I will negotiate a separation and a divorce agreement," said Benowitz. "But first, I have to establish a rapport with the other lawyer representing your husband to hammer out terms of an agreement."

"It's sounds pretty complicated."

"It involves a lot of meetings and sometimes letters."

"What happens if the two sides cannot come to an agreement?"

Benowitz looked stern. "Then the case is litigated in court. A judge becomes involved.

"But judges in matrimonial cases are reluctant to help with the terms of the settlement; they generally persuade the parties involved along with their lawyers to come to an agreement, regarding alimony and child support, and the distribution of assets."

It was possible for the court to stipulate that Abbie occupy the house for a certain period of time, say, while the children were growing up. Once the children went on to college, the house would be turned over to the owner.

Dan explained that in the eyes of the law, her children were considered of "tender age" and there was no question of custody. In 1975 the mother almost always got sole custody of young children. Unless the court deemed the mother to be an unfit mother.

Abbie shuddered at the suggestion.

Dan went on, "It's all about money. Your divorce is going to be all about the money; how much money is the big question."

Before Abbie left, Benowitz told her to go home and try to discuss the question of money with Sam.

"Ask him how much support money he wants to give you, since he wants the divorce."

That night, when Sam came home and was looking through his things in the bedroom closet, Abbie confronted him.

"Let's talk for a moment." She told him she had a lawyer and that she had met with him that day.

"You want a divorce, I understand, and there's nothing I can do about that. But how are we going to get by? How much support are you going to provide for me and the children?"

He turned to her, as he was undoing his carefully knotted tie, and he yelled in her face, "You can't get blood out of a stone."

Abbie saw a blue vein pop on his forehead and his eyes blazed. Little flecks of green flashed in his hazel eyes.

"You are asking me about money. I'm going to tell you how much you will get, not some lawyer or a judge. I'll take care of my children, but I don't intend to take care of you."

Abbie was thunderstruck.

Sam had been sporadically giving her the weekly allowance of $278 for household expenses and the housekeeper. He continued to pay for utilities and mortgage and taxes on his house.

The next day, Abbie called Benowitz and when he called her back later that night, she told him what Sam had said about the money.

"We are going to have to try and get him out of the house. This is all going to take a lot of time. So be patient."

Chapter Thirty-Two

Around town, Abbie tried to put on a positive face, going to her weekly tennis game, shopping for food, and taking a class at the high school. One of her neighbors who was a close friend stopped talking to her after running into Sam on the train. He told her he wanted to be a tycoon and that Abbie was crushing his ambition.

Jennifer, who had hosted the baby shower, continued to be her friend and invited her to parties. But when she told Dan Benowitz they smoked pot, he forbade her to go.

"That's just the kind of thing the lawyer will be looking for. Behavior that makes you an unfit mother." Dan said.

One bright morning, a neighbor rang her bell. Abbie saw it was Marilyn Goldstein, a neighbor from up the street. They rarely socialized but knew each other from the school. Her husband, Jerry Goldstein, was a wealthy man who was totally blind. He had gotten custody of his young daughter when he and his first wife divorced. He later married Marilyn, a plain-looking, but very nice woman. They had a little boy who was in Eve's class and a new baby boy.

"Abbie, "she said, "I had to get over here and tell you something important. This morning, Jerry's old detective, Fred French, the guy he used during his divorce, rang our bell to ask me if he could use our bathroom. I was surprised to see him. I asked him what he was doing in the neighborhood and he told me he was watching some woman named Cooperman."

It turned out that French was Sonny Heller's private eye. Heller was a bomber divorce lawyer in New York.

The second time that Abbie went to Dan's office, he told her that Sam had changed lawyers and had retained Heller to handle the divorce. Heller's tactics were to carry on a siege, through a protracted divorce, attempting to wear down the wife and get her to "fold," as Benowitz termed it.

"We are not going to fold," became Dan's litany. "We are fighting for the rest of your life."

As weeks passed, Sam stayed in the house. He went to work and came home late. Since there was no Separation Agreement or formal visitation arrangements, he could just grab the children whenever he wanted and take them for the day or weekend or do whatever he liked.

It dawned on Abbie that divorce negotiations could go on and on, even for years — to her, this represented forever.

Benowitz stressed again, "We have to get your husband out of the house. The only way is by alleging violence."

Alleging violence? That's pretty dramatic. "No," she said, he has never been violent with me. Although he hits our daughter."

After Abbie heard about detective French and how Jerry Goldstein had gotten custody, she started to panic. Months went by, an endless stream of letters were exchanged between Benowitz and Heller, filled with accusations and threats of motions. Abbie was going to her lawyer's office at least once a week and talking to him on the phone every day and at night.

The day that the Summons and Complaint was submitted, Abbie knew with certainty that Sam was going to make custody an issue. Dan explained that custody was a legal ploy to intimidate her.

In the Complaint, Sam alleged that Abbie was an unfit mother. The formal document read: "Abbie spends very little time with the children. She plays tennis and goes to lunches while the housekeeper takes care of Sara, Lila, and Eve. Sometimes Abbie strikes the children."

On the day she walked into Dan's office to read the Complaint, he was sitting at his desk smoking a cigarette. He said, "Do you know what your husband is? He's a fucking asshole."

Abbie started to shake.

"Dan, he's unfit," she said, trembling. "He's never home, and when he is, he hits my daughter. My mother has seen him hit the children."

"We have to prove it. We must get you some money, a divorce, and a new life."

The cigarette dangled from his lips as he stared at her.

Chapter Thirty-Three
The Reign of Terror

Sam's second lawyer, Sidney "Sonny" Heller, was a matrimonial lawyer so fiercely litigious that he was called a "bomber." His strategy was to wear down the opposing side, that usually being the wife.

Abbie had learned that equitable distribution was somewhere in the future. In New York, and most other states, women had few legal rights under matrimonial law and had to depend on the good will of their husbands.

Dan said, "Sam has the upper hand because he has his own business and is able to hide his income and assets. We have to hope that he will be fair and reasonable. You have three young children. He's been the breadwinner in the marriage and is expected to support you."

"What does that mean?" Abbie said. "Will we be able to stay in our house?"

"I doubt that. Because the house is in his name. Heller is going to try and wear you down so you will settle for less. Under duress, he thinks you will fold, as most women do."

The campaign to wear Abbie down began with disparaging letters that two or three times a week were sent to Benowitz. The correspondence was all about Abbie's weaknesses and failure to take proper care of her children. The papers went back and forth until a foot-high stack of onion skin accusations had accumulated on Dan's untidy desk.

"More letters from Heller," Dan said. "It will end, I promise you."

Every time she read a new letter, Abbie was sick to her stomach.

"He's setting the stage for making me an unfit mother," she told her mother in Chicago.

"It looks that way," Bessie said. "I never liked him."

One night when Sam came home, Abbie meekly approached him.

"You wanted a divorce. Why can't we do this amicably?"

Sam glared at her and walked away.

In her sleep that night, Abbie dreamt that Sam would keep all his money, his house, and get custody. He would toss her aside like garbage. She envisioned his second wife taking over as the mother of her children. Her greatest fear was that his money could buy the judges, that his tenacity would wipe her out and leave her a lonely beggar, groveling to see her children.

"You will end up with nothing," said the troll in her sleep.

Abbie had few people to talk to about what was happening…the horror of it all. Carol, her best friend, said, "People think of divorce as a contagious disease and they don't want to catch it."

To top off the terror, anonymous phone calls began coming in every day at 3 p.m., the time that the kids came home from school.

"No one speaks. Just silence," Abbie told her mother. "I think it's my in-laws trying to scare me."

"They want to see if you're home for the kids," Bessie said. "If you are not there, they can accuse you of being a neglectful mother."

After two weeks of silent phone calls, Manny, her father-in-law, said in the latest call, "It's time for you to leave, go live in your parents' one-bedroom apartment in Florida."

Abbie had heard about women without means fighting for their children against wealthy husbands who financed protracted divorce proceedings, cases where the women could not endure the mental stress and anguish. They would be broken financially and emotionally and forced to walk away, or give up and settle for unfair terms

Sad news went around town about a woman named Barbara. Shy and quiet, Abbie knew her from school where her son was in second grade with Lila. She had endured a nightmarish split-up that went to court because the couple failed to come to terms. The husband sued for custody of their three young children while he harassed his wife by making negative accusations about her behavior. Even worse, he was withholding temporary child support payments ordered by the court.

During the summer at the town pool, Abbie met Barbara. She had dark circles under her eyes and the look of uneasiness. They talked quietly under a tree near the main swimming pool.

"Hi, Barbara, how are you doing? Are the kids going to camp?"

"My mother came to help me. It's a difficult time…as you probably know," Barbara said.

Her husband was making her look like an unfit mother. My heart ached for her, but I couldn't get too involved because I was in trouble myself.

Barbara claimed that during the divorce her husband had installed voice recorders in their house, a mansion in the estate section of town, and excerpted private conversations to try and malign her. After two years of fighting over money and custody, the divorce was settled in court. The judge awarded Barbara sole custody of the children and a modicum of child support. Her husband lived in the city with his girlfriend.

Barbara and the kids moved to a small house in Pleasantville, but the husband withheld child support and she had to resort to welfare. That following winter, Abbie heard through the grapevine that poor Barbara had committed suicide.

"She couldn't take it anymore," said a close friend. "Her monster of an ex-husband, a psychiatrist in Manhattan, knew how to break her."

Abbie's neighbor said, "The system failed her. She felt helpless and couldn't afford to continuously go back to court for money."

"Doesn't anybody enforce the payments?" Abbie asked. Her neighbor shrugged.

Abbie was learning how the legal system operated in New York, still a title state in the 1970s, before changes to equitable distribution of property. Justice was meted in favor of the party with the most expensive cunning lawyer and the one who could stay the course the longest. Custody threats and custody battles, she learned, were merely legal ploys to get women to settle, to accept less money, or to give up entirely.

"Heller is trying to pressure you by denigrating your character," Benowitz said. Other lawyers in the firm cheered her on and voiced the same opinion. "You won't lose your children."

They kept telling her there was no possibility of losing custody.

But what if she lost her strong and competent attorney? What if he deserted her, too, like her husband?

As the case dragged on throughout the summer and into the fall, Abbie became more impressed by Benowitz' charm and wit, and more emotionally involved. He always had some joke to tell her. He made fun of Sam, calling him a dunce.

"How's the dunce? Is he still sleeping in the playroom? Can he hear you giggling?"

"Yes, he just came in and gave me a dirty look," Abbie said.

"Don't worry, we will win this case," Dan said. "You will have a life, I promise."

Every Saturday night, home alone, Abbie got a call from Benowitz. "I'm out getting the *New York Times*. It is starting to get cold. How are you doing, Abbie girl?"

The kids were asleep upstairs. The baby was going to get her last bottle at midnight.

"I'm okay. Very anxious."

His voice calmed her. *He is my gift from heaven.*

Still, she felt like she was in a bind, depending on him for her life.

In her diary, she wrote: *I'm being hurt by my husband, but I could also get hurt by my lawyer. I'm in a double bind.*

One afternoon in the city, Benowitz took her out for lunch. It was a local deli around the corner from his office in midtown Manhattan where a lot of garment center types and their secretaries hung out.

They ordered tuna sandwiches on rye and potato chips. Dan ordered a coke and she had a chocolate egg cream. The place was noisy as a factory, but no one knew them. No one glanced their way. They were two friends having a bite.

They talked about marriage and divorce. "Look, Abbie, most of the time, men hold the purse strings. They retain high-priced, cagey lawyers like me who file motion after motion. I worked for a family court judge for seven years, so I know the process, and it's crooked.

"Judges don't really want to force agreements, they don't have the capacity to force fair settlements. They rely on the lawyers to make agreements."

"I thought we could go to court and the judge would see how cruel Sam has been," Abbie said. "Can't we go to trial?"

"Judges always try to push for settlements and if that fails, there could be a trial. Trials are very expensive, though, so matrimonial trials are unusual."

He paused, then said, "Abbie, I swear to you, I will stand by you and get you as fair an agreement as possible. You will get custody of your children,

"You will have enough money to get by, but you will have to get a job."

He took her hand and held it. They looked at each other raptly, the way old friends, or devoted lovers, hold their gazes.

Abbie was oblivious to the chatter and crashing dishes as she got lost in Dan's sweet and steady expression.

"I am confident that we will prevail," he said. "Do you trust me?"

"Yes, I do."

As the legal process continued and worsened, anxiety consumed her. During the day, she forced herself to eat. At night, she sat with the kids at dinner and got them ready for bed. She talked on the phone to a few friends, always conscious of how much to tell them.

"Don't trust anyone," said her mother.

Dan's efforts to settle the divorce amicably with Heller were met with threats and accusations, setting the groundwork for court intervention.

Dan had said at the beginning, "This is all scare tactics. Heller makes his money by litigating, not by negotiating. If your husband had the right lawyer, we could talk it all out, and come to terms about alimony and child support. But a bomber like Heller wants to argue and intimidate, so that the wife will settle for next to nothing."

After putting the baby to bed, Abbie tossed and turned in her bed at night, tortured by the suspense, and her unknown future. Sam had adored her for years, or seemed to. He dressed her in couture clothes from Paris and surprised her with diamond hearts on Valentine's Day.

Why was he so determined now to discard her, to break her down through intimidation and litigation?

Abbie's mother was the first to say it. *There's another woman.*

"He wants you to have a nervous breakdown. Then he can have his house and his children, and all his money," Bessie said. "He wants to get you out of his life."

Abbie's mother did not mean to be cruel. She just saw things that other people did not, and she said, "It's becoming clear he has some woman who is quite prepared to step into your place as mother and wife."

Abbie was spending at least one day a week in the lawyer's office. She couldn't tell anyone how she felt about Dan, but she knew she really looked to being with him.

They would chat. Dan would always ask about the children and learned about her best friend Carol. "Don't trust her," he said.

Then they would read new damning letters from Heller, who was always dropping verbal bombs and accusations about Abbie's behavior.

One letter stated: "My client does not intend to pay alimony. Mrs. Cooperman is a teacher by education and she can get a job and support herself."

Another letter said: "Mrs. Cooperman does not take care of the children. She leaves all the work for the housekeeper while she goes to play tennis."

The worst letter was about custody: "Mr. Cooperman is asking for full custody of the three children. He has the means to take care of them and his parents, who reside in New York, are willing and able to provide child care."

Sitting in Dan's dreary office with the blinds half-closed, Abbie cried momentarily, but quickly regained her composure.

She said, "This custody issue isn't going to go away. This case could go on for years. And I haven't been able to pay you a dime. What would I do without you?"

"All right, listen," said Dan. "I want to play you a song by someone you might not know." He turned on his cassette player and she heard Carole King's music for the first time.

The lyrics started, and for the first time, she really listened to *You've Got a Friend*.

Tears fell down her cheeks.

Dan winked at her. "Listen and don't forget these words,"

During the darkest days of 1975 and 1976, that song became her litany, her mainstay, while Benowitz was her pillar of strength. She recalled their first meeting, when she had walked into his office wearing her Diane Von Furstenberg wrap dress.

Over the ensuing months of motions and threats, Abbie's future hinged on Dan Benowitz's legal moves and maneuvers. Her lawyer became her rock, her champion, *and* her lover.

Chapter Thirty-Four

At their first meeting, Benowitz had said, "Your children are so young and that's what makes your case unusual. The law describes them of tender age. Although you are married for seven years, the court does not consider it a long marriage.

"But there are state laws and in New York you are entitled to alimony and child support. Maybe a lump sum, if we can find your husband's assets. But I doubt it.

"Do you have any funds of your own?"

"I have a $5,000 bond that my father-in-law bought for me. Sam gives me an allowance of $278 a week and he pays for everything else."

Benowitz scratched his head and reached for a cigarette. His glass ashtray was already filled with butts.

The sun was streaming through the dusty windows in his cramped office. Manilla folders were piled here and there on the floor behind his desk.

Abbie could see his brain working. *He knows Sam is wealthy and can pay the bill in the final outcome.*

She had read about divorce in the newspaper. How divorce lawyers were awarded hefty sums of money. A friend told her that legal fees could be included in the divorce settlement.

"This case is a lot of work and will take a long time, because of the money involved. And I don't know how long it will take to settle the case… but honestly…you and I have a mutual friend who sent you here. I do sometimes take pro bono cases. So, I'm willing to work for you.

"You should understand, however, there are extraneous costs involved and my office can't be responsible for all of it."

Abbie's mind was drifting. But she heard him say there were court fees, administrative costs for secretaries, and document copying, which Abbie would owe him. The pages of letters and legal motions eventually filled an entire filing cabinet. At some point in the future, Abbie would have to raise some money for these out-of-pocket fees. Although Dan didn't press her, she thought of a way to get some money.

"Let's go steal a car," Abbie said one night to Carol. They took five of the children in Carol's station wagon and drove to the Bronx. Abbie's mother-in-law was in possession of the car, and there it was parked in front of Grandma's house.

"Are we going to visit Grandma?" Eve asked.

"Not tonight, honey," Abbie said. "Mommy needs her car back."

Abbie was not in the habit of stealing cars, especially at night, but it did belong to her. By then she had learned all about title, and the title of the car was in her name, so it belonged to her.

"I feel like I'm stealing the car," Abbie said to Carol, "but it's mine."

She got out of Carol's station wagon and walked up to her VW hatchback. She hadn't driven it in months. Sam had given it to his mother.

She cautiously opened the car door with her set of keys, got behind the wheel, turned on the ignition, and waved to Carol and the kids. As they had pre-planned, she pulled out of the space and drove away.

Like a thief in the night.

Carol and the kids followed her back to Pleasantville.

She sold her hatchback to a friend for $2800. That was how she got the money to pay Dan for out-of-pocket legal expenses.

Abbie was the Plaintiff in the lawsuit. In the papers that Benowitz drew up, she sued Sam, the Defendant, for divorce and custody of the children. Sole custody. Dan would negotiate temporary alimony and child support and a reasonable visitation schedule for when Sam could see the children.

Benowitz told her what to expect. "The key to settling the case is by negotiating with the opposing lawyer to reach a fair and equitable agreement in regard to alimony and child support. First, we are seeking Temporary Alimony and Child Support, while the case is hammered out. Because right now, you are only getting $278 a week.

"A Separation Agreement would then be drawn up by one of the lawyers. Eventually, that agreement would merge with the final divorce decree. It could take months before you can go on with your life.

"Whatever funds and benefits we can get for you during this critical period will shape your future as the children grow up, and even beyond. Once a divorce is final, it can be financially prohibitive to go back to court to make a plea for additional alimony or child support.

"Practically speaking, what we are able to get now will indicate what the final divorce agreement will contain."

As he puffed on his Parliament, he tried to educate Abbie. "Temporary alimony and child support, called *Pendente Lite*, will set the tone for the case going forward."

The agreement that would be forged had to include all the necessities that the children might require in the future: dental care and braces, sleepaway camp, and college. There also remained the question of private school if Abbie wanted to move back to the city. But at the time she was unable to think that far ahead.

Several months were wasted getting on track with the case while Heller remained Sam's lawyer. Abbie collected information about New York "bomber" lawyers. Heller held a prominent position at the top of the list.

In his book *Divorce*, Raoul Felder, a renowned New York City divorce attorney, discussed some hair-raising techniques of the trade. One anecdote told of a prince who hired a gigolo to seduce his wife, then hired a band of private detectives to capture several moments of indiscretion on film.

On this note, Benowitz warned Abbie not to open the door to strangers, who might jump her while a photographer took pictures that looked like adultery. In fact, Sam did bribe their long-time live-in housekeeper to keep a diary on Abbie's activities. She told Abbie about Sam's approach to her and her refusal to be an informant.

"The divorce business is indeed ruthless, brutal, and filled with as much ugliness as the human psyche can conjure up," according to Charles Sopkin, who reviewed

Felder's book in 1974. "Bombers are in business to accommodate hate. Like Doberman pinschers, they get directly to the heart of the matter..."

The fight was going to be tough. *Men who own private businesses can hide income, usually offshore, and they use business revenues for company cars, entertainment, life insurance, or petty cash. For almost anything.*

In 1975, women with children were legally entitled to alimony and child support. For someone like Sam, alimony was appealing since it was a tax deduction. The recipient, usually the mother, had to pay taxes on alimony. Child support was not a tax deduction. If the mother received child support, she paid no taxes on the money, since the funds are used for the care of the children.

"Alimony is taxable, child support, tax free," Benowitz explained. "For Sam, in a high-income bracket, alimony is a highly negotiable component of the agreement. Sam will prefer to pay more alimony than child support, so he can use it as a tax advantage."

Prior to the Equitable Distribution Law in New York State, enacted July 19, 1980, there were no concrete rules about alimony. Some judges worked out alimony and child support to be worth 40 percent of a man's gross income. Or the estimate might be to take one-third to one-half of after-tax income as the basis of determining alimony and child support. In most cases that involved middle class families; both parties were often left with hardly enough money to live on.

Abbie really didn't know exactly how much Sam earned, except for the last tax return she had signed in 1974. His gross income then was $125,000, a sizable amount at the time. Dan suspected that Sam might have offshore accounts, which Abbie knew nothing about.

Thirty years passed before she actually found out.

One morning in late spring of 1975, Benowitz boarded the train up to White Plains, the county seat. Abbie met him at the Westchester County courthouse, where he planned to file a Motion for Divorce. They climbed up the steep stone steps of the stately building, walked through the austere marble corridors, and into the clerk's office. Dan started to fill out forms, but abruptly, he turned to Abbie. She could see his brain working and then he spoke softly, "I don't think we should be filing in Westchester County. You're both residents here but it would be better if we filed in New York County.

"I don't know why I didn't think of this before. Come on, let's go outside and I'll tell you something." He took Abbie's elbow and led her out of the grand hall.

"Don't ever repeat this," he said, as they stood in the middle of downtown White Plains, an ordinary suburban town acting as the seat of county government. "You know, before I went into private practice, I clerked for a judge in New York Supreme Court. For seven years.

"That could help us. I know people in the Manhattan courts."

He explained to Abbie that judges in New York Supreme Court tended to award more money to women than judges in the Westchester County Court. The decision was made, and over the next few days, Dan filed the lawsuit for divorce in New York Supreme Court. It stayed there, too, because Heller, Sam's lawyer, never asked for a change of venue. He overlooked the fact that his client resided in Westchester, where he might have gotten a sweeter deal.

Chapter Thirty-Five
Serving Sam

The next step in the divorce process was Service. A processor had to serve Sam with a Summons with notice that Abbie was filing for divorce. Technically, the Defendant had to accept the Notice. Abbie remembered seeing this type of action on television and in the movies. The defendant always looks surprised when the papers are being thrust into his hand. But then, the defendant invariably takes the papers.

Just as Abbie's mother always preached, treacherous things were happening. It seemed logical that Sam would go along with the divorce process, since he wanted the divorce so much. But instead, he was going to make it difficult, placing obstacles along every step of the way. That was the bomber's strategy: intimidation, posturing, and protraction. The game's singular objective was about wearing the opponent down and even causing the other lawyer to fire his client. Sam figured that no lawyer is going to work his tail off for a woman who has no money to pay him.

"You can be sure I'm never going to pay for your lawyer," Sam said to Abbie one night when they were arguing about money. "As I told you, it will be me who decides what you get not some judge."

Sam never forgot his young years in a labor camp during the war. When they got to America, his mother and father peddled second-hand clothes and saved every nickel they could earn. No husband ever wants to pay his wife's legal fees, and Sam's life would have to be threatened before he would do what the system said.

"This is going to be a long and protracted case to wear you down, and me, so that I will quit. But I won't, I promise. I won't leave you," Dan swore earnestly, gently placing his hand on her shoulder.

Dan started to call Abbie day and night and on weekends to prop her up.

Later when the lawsuit heated up, he instructed her to always call him from a phone booth at the Pleasantville train station in the village. He was convinced that the phones in the house were tapped.

Benowitz started to call her "AC" and he would say, "How are you doing, AC? Just remember you *will* have a life."

In the dark depressing days that would follow, when she would be giving baby Sara a bottle at midnight watching TV in the den, Abbie would think about the silly stuff Dan said to keep up her spirits.

Dan read to her from, *Horton Hatches the Egg* by Dr. Seuss, a book he always read to one of his young daughters. When he sensed that Abbie was frightened, he would give her the lines from the book.

"I said what I meant and I meant what I said, an elephant's faithful one hundred percent."

In that first year of Sara's life, while Abbie cared for her and the other two young girls, Dan worked on the case, drafting letters back and forth to Heller about how Sam was harassing her, coming and going as he pleased and alleging that he had a girlfriend. In all the papers, the wording stressed that the children were of "tender age."

Sam had still not been successfully served, however. Every time the processor went to Sam's office on Broadway, he would be turned away by the receptionist. Or if he caught Sam in the hall, the papers were refused, and Sam would quickly get away. There were rules about Service, so the processor could not actually force the papers on him. Weeks and months went by and they couldn't get the case off the ground.

Sam was preparing for one of his business trips to Taiwan and that would mean the divorce would be in limbo for weeks until he returned, and they would have to start all over again trying to make him accept the papers.

Benowitz devised an elaborate plan. He contacted a lawyer in Taipei and told him about the American husband who wanted to divorce his wife who had just given birth to their baby and he was avoiding service. The Taiwanese lawyer was sympathetic and agreed to arrange for Sam to be served with divorce papers at the hotel. One day while Sam was having breakfast at the President Hotel in Taipei, where the couple had stayed together for months, he was served with papers. The lawyer told them that when the processor approached Sam and thrust the papers in his hand while he was eating his breakfast in a foreign country, he looked shocked. But that was not enough because Benowitz wanted to make sure that this time the service would stick.

When Sam came home from the Far East, Dan went up to Westchester and they found Sam's car parked at the service station across from the Pleasantville train. They waited for him to get off the train and Dan approached him and thrust the papers at him.

"Are you Sam Cooperman?" he said. The surprise of it all was overwhelming. Sam was left holding the papers. Abbie had a camera with her and took a picture of Dan handing him the documents. He had finally been served!

New York Supreme Court recognized the Service that was performed in Taipei. Officially the divorce suit was titled: Cooperman v. Cooperman.

Abbie was formally suing Sam for divorce on the grounds of cruel and inhuman treatment and constructive abandonment, the latter meaning he refused to have sexual relations with her.

In July, when Sara was five months old, the New York Supreme Court accepted that service had been rendered and the divorce process was commenced. In the first few months, when it looked like her case for divorce was going to stand up in court, Sam called Abbie.

She was surprised to hear his voice…a gentle voice that she remembered from their dating days.

"Abbie, let's not do this. It has gone too far. I really don't want to get a divorce. Let's work this out."

Abbie was shocked. She wrote in her diary: *Sam had never thought I could get this going and that a tough smart lawyer was on my side.*

She agreed to have dinner with him in downtown White Plains at a little French bistro that had been a favorite. Over a candlelit meal, he used his many charms trying to persuade her to discharge Benowitz and work things out between them with the possibility of reconciliation.

"I've been thinking about our marriage," Sam spoke softly. He looked sad and weak.

"Let's put all this behind us and get back together. For the sake of the children."

Abbie didn't say a word. She sat silently, forcing herself to keep her expression blank, but inwardly stunned.

"Your lawyer is just using you to run up the bill," he went on.

He kept sticking a fork into the green beans on his plate. "You are making a big mistake, I'm telling you."

Back then, Sam was still eating meat. The sauce on his boeuf bourguignon was congealed. "You get more with honey than with vinegar," he said, not looking at her. His black lashes fluttered against his tawny skin; a shadow of a beard on his sculptured face. She clenched a fist in her lap.

That was the first time, but not the last time, that Sam would malign Dan and try to pit them against each other. He wanted Abbie to second guess herself. And she did many times, almost ruining her relationship with Benowitz.

"I'll think about it," Abbie said. "You've already caused me so much pain. How can I believe you? I want to believe you, would like to get back together." And she wept at the table.

When they parted, Sam looked forlorn. Abbie drove home alone to her children.

When she told Dan about the conversation, he was outraged. "If you go back to him, everything that we have accomplished will be undone. You will be condoning everything that he has done to you."

Undoubtedly, it was a trick, which she had inwardly known. In her heart, she yearned to believe that Sam really wanted to get back together, to come back to his beautiful young family. How nice it would have been to regain her old life, even though she was lonely. It was sad, tragic, debilitating. But there was no way back. The severe damage had been done, she was deeply wounded, incredibly devastated by his actions and cruelty. There was going to be a divorce.

Or so she thought. The next trick Sam and his attorney pulled out of their hat was to contest the divorce.

The divorce that he started, that he wanted…now he's fighting it. Contesting it to put me in limbo.

In reply papers, a response to the Complaint, Sam stated that he had never actually wanted a divorce. Dan told her it was a simple strategy, a ploy of Sonny Heller's, and one that could work. If the courts denied her petition for divorce, her life could be in limbo for years. If Sam remained her husband, she would always be under surveillance. If she started to go out with friends or on dates, she could be deemed an unfit mother. She would be stuck, deeply and completely stuck.

Chapter Thirty-Six

The summer after Sara was born, the word got out all over town that Abbie Cooperman was getting a divorce. Acquaintances stared at her in the supermarket. Most of her friends stopped calling. She was *persona non grata* in Pleasantville.

"I feel like the maiden with the scarlet letter," she told her high school friend Roz who lived in Los Angeles.

Always prone to feeling self-conscious, Abbie forced herself to put on make-up and go about her errands in the village. She did her usual chores, shopping, and taking the children to the community pool where she would see half the people in town lounging in chairs and on blankets, eating at the snack bar, and checking out who looked good in a bathing suit. She felt very exposed, indeed.

I'm not going to hide or be ashamed, she wrote in her diary. *My children are here with me and I have a few friends who care.*

It wasn't like everyone was talking about her, but many were, especially Brigitte Miller and her friends from the bridge club. Now she was not just that horrible person, she was that young mother getting a divorce, which in 1975 was still a rare occurrence in Pleasantville.

Besides loneliness and constant anxiety that affected her appetite, Abbie felt a profound loss of identity. She was no longer the wife of the successful businessman, Sam Cooperman. She was going to lose the title of Mrs., a chilling prospect. She was becoming the character she played in her parents' messy bedroom when she was 10, a single mother of orphaned children alone in the forest with no place to live.

She took great comfort from Benowitz's attention — his phone calls, his wry jokes and stories in his office, many late in the evening. And his verbal stabs at Sam, who he nicknamed "Sneaky Sneaker Man."

One day when she stayed in town while Dan followed up on phone messages, he emerged from his cluttered desk to say good-bye and comfort her. They had gotten another disheartening letter about disclosure.

"Sam is refusing to submit personal financial records to the court, a mandatory procedure," Dan said. "He is putting himself above the law."

"Can he get away with this?"

"It's a rule that he must disclose his income and assets. He's definitely stalling."

Benowitz stood close to Abbie and put his hand on her shoulder. "Stay a little longer," he whispered. "Do you have to go right back home?"

Then, "I'd really like to kiss you. May I?"

Uh, oh, she thought. Before Abbie said a word, Dan kissed her softly on the lips and she didn't move.

She stood there frozen, then guardedly looked into his eyes.

"We could get in trouble, right? This is unethical. Illegal?"

"Yes. But I can't help it. I swear to you, I have never, ever done this before, with a client."

Abbie never expected to enjoy his kisses. He was scruffy, smoked cigarettes, and was not classically handsome.

In her diary she wrote, *I find him irresistible; his personality and conversation make up for everything. Not only does he have a brilliant, witty mind, he is empathetic and kind.*

One scorching summer afternoon, after they had worked on her case, and he read her excerpts from disturbing, accusing letters that could pave the wave to a serious custody suit, he asked her if she would like to go for a drive. She had the day to herself since the kids were in day camp and her parents and the housekeeper were taking care of the baby.

"I have a studio apartment uptown where it's cool and we can get away from business," Dan said.

Abbie smoothed her lemon-colored cotton tee shirt and floral wrap skirt that tied at the side of her waist. The yellow, green, pink, and violet colors made her feel happy. Dan took her hand and they taxied uptown and entered a doorman building. The apartment was simple and cozy, but it looked like no one lived there. For once, Benowitz was quiet, quickly embracing her.

"I've been wanting to hold you," he said, kissing her softly. That's when they made love for the first time.

Abbie felt that she deserved every pleasurable minute. They lay on the thick shag rug of the orderly studio, and he held her while he opened the side of her cottony wrap skirt to lightly touch her.

It was the only time they ever spent in that apartment. Instead, they started to meet in Yonkers at a shopping mall parking lot, where it was easier to be discreet.

"I love you," he told her. They cherished a few hours talking and cuddling in her gray Mercedes, the car that was in her name.

Between kisses, they would make jokes about the legal battle. Sam was still a part-time occupant, though they had little discourse.

Benowitz would jest about the self-proclaimed tycoon who made up his own rules: "Is he still eating your cooking? Does he like sleeping in the playroom? Does he still want you to shine his shoes?

"If he ever tries to hurt you in any way, we can include violence in the legal papers."

Poking fun at Sam's egotisms and idiosyncratic behavior, and the opposing lawyers' legal machinations — put things in a comical perspective. She giggled thinking of the ploys and games, like juvenile high school antics.

One night when Sam came home late, hanging out in the playroom, he heard her on the phone laughing.

"What are you doing? Are you talking to your lawyer? You are probably sleeping with him. Tell me, what's going on with you two?"

"That is ludicrous," Abbie shouted. "You are the one who is cheating and deserting your family."

I can't believe I said that. I'm learning from Dan.

There was no one that Abbie could trust to discuss her affair. She never told Carol, her best friend, who asked many curious questions.

In fact, Abbie never told anyone about her affair with Dan until years later. By then she had learned that having an affair with your divorce lawyer was not unusual.

Abbie believed that Dan's feelings for her were real and she adored him. She was not in love the way she had been in love with Marty.

Their trips to the parking lot in Yonkers continued. When Abbie got home after dark, Bessie would be waiting up.

Without asking questions, Bessie said, "You are playing with fire. I hope you know what you're doing. Too much is happening. You could have a nervous breakdown."

If I lose my children, that could happen.

"Mom, I'm OK, I am not going to have a nervous breakdown."

"Sam could trick you. And I wouldn't trust your lawyer either. They could be in cahoots."

On the legal front, the case was headed for court. A hearing was scheduled for the lawyers to appear before the judge. They couldn't come to an agreement, especially on the matter of financials. Sam refused to disclose his earnings and assets. Heller was still on Sam's side, sending scurrilous letters back and forth. Dan accused him of "obfuscating" the issues that needed to be resolved: support, custody, and visitation.

There was nothing on the table. And all Abbie was getting was $278 a week for household expenses.

But the one critical issue that Heller failed to address, or even mention in correspondence, was the matter of venue. He had not asked for a change of venue. He forgot or was really not that interested in Sam's case. Maybe he wasn't paying him enough. Sam was rich, but not Rockefeller rich.

For that reason, the case was played out in Manhattan, New York County, where Benowitz knew all the judges and many of the clerks.

Still, the custody issue hung over Abbie like a shroud. No matter that she was a good mother. Every lawyer in Dan's office told her not to worry about custody.

"It's all about the money," they kept saying.

The case dragged on throughout the summer. Abbie didn't think that they would ever come to an agreement. Months went by with no progress. Dan believed that they would eventually go to trial, and that a judge would have to step in and force the terms of an agreement.

Abbie pictured herself taking the witness stand in court. They would request a jury, Benowitz said dramatically.

I can imagine wearing a tailored gray suit and a white blouse, and small black heels.

She looked at herself in the mirror. Pearl earrings, small ones, barely noticeable. She would cut her hair to a medium length and wear muted make-up.

Abbie's problem-solving skills came to the surface. Eve was now seven years old and in a Brownie troop at school. They needed a leader. Abbie volunteered to run the Brownie troop beginning in September.

No one takes away children from a Brownie leader. She clung to that thought for comfort. She could wear her Brownie leader uniform in front of preliminary hearings in court. At trial, she would wear the gray suit and white blouse.

Throughout the summer, she made sure to be seen in a one-piece bathing suit at the Pleasantville pool, always with her three children in tow and sometimes the mother's helper. The children took swimming lessons. She never went out socially. Sam kept coming and going as he pleased and often he would take the children on Sundays.

Sam and his father would march into the house and hurriedly grab Eve and Lila and a knapsack with clothing items and a few toys, leaving the baby at home.

Benowitz hatched a plan. "We are going to teach them a lesson. One Sunday, I want you to get up very early and take the children to one of your friends and disappear for the entire day. When Sam comes marching in with Manny, and nobody is home, that will really rile them up. They won't be too happy about that."

Abbie's parents were in town and they prepared for this mission, loading up diaper bags and cold drinks, baby biscuits, and peanut butter sandwiches. By 8 a.m. on a Sunday in July, they drove off and headed north to the Tappan Zee Bridge and over to the New Jersey side to Abbie's friend Judy Fenton's house in northern Jersey. She had a baby the same age as Sara and her son and Eve had been playmates in Manhattan, before they all moved to the suburbs.

They stayed the entire day, talked about the divorce and old times. Judy made a barbecue for the six children, until at last, Abbie put everyone in the car and drove back to Pleasantville.

It was dark. The house was empty and silent. About 9 p.m., the phone rang breaking the quiet; it was Manny. In his deep heavily accented voice, he said slowly and deliberately, "Abbie, we have powerful cameras watching you."

Abbie's heart was pounding as she stood in the kitchen warming a bottle for Sara. Then slowly, she said in a trembling voice, "Listen, Manny, I'm not the one who wanted this divorce. It's your son."

The old man answered, "If my son wants a divorce, it must be for a reason. It must be for a reason, there is a reason."

For a reason…a reason. The phrase echoed in Abbie's brain for the next year and a half.

But on that night, she hung up and checked all the window shades and blinds, swallowed a Valium and went to bed. In the middle of the night, Eve came into her mother's bedroom and quietly lay down beside her.

Chapter Thirty-Seven
In Limbo

By the autumn of 1975, Abbie was desperate for funds to live on. The allowance that Sam was sending did not cover her household expenses for food, childcare, and clothing.

Sam had cut off their credit cards, all in his name. No more Saks Fifth Avenue or Bloomingdales.

This is what happens when you depend on a man. I have no identity.

The rotting front lawn upset Abbie the most. It had turned from green to dry brown weeds from a fungus that required a special treatment. It was an eyesore, a daily reminder of something else she did not have the money to fix or erase.

Sam was making mortgage payments and taxes because he owned the house, but Abbie could barely afford the other essentials, including Ginger, the housekeeper, whom Sam had bribed to get a diary about her activities. Ginger said she refused the offer.

I either believe her or fire her, which might make matters worse. Again, Abbie felt caught in a bind.

Then Abbie heard about a teaching assistant job at a school in Irvington. The teacher of the deaf in charge of the school's resource room needed an assistant for three days a week.

"We tutor eight hearing-impaired students who attend regular classes, but they need extra help," Susan Morris, the lead teacher said. "The kids, who vary in ages from kindergarten through sixth grade, are very bright with good speech and language skills."

Susan hired Abbie to work three days a week in her resource room. Soon they became fast friends. Abbie trusted her and confided in her.

"My lawyer found out that there is another woman," Abbie told her.

"That figures. How did he find out?"

"He got hold of some telephone records that listed an international phone number on the bill. Sam has been calling the number frequently. The woman lives in Tokyo. She's a likely candidate."

Her name was Mia and she worked for the company that finances Sam's projects. Could her mother have been right? Had an exotic Asian woman seduced him?

"It's not surprising. He's over there all the time," Susan said. "Whoever she is, she is a novelty for him."

"He never seemed to show interest in that type of woman. The calls started in early 1974, right before I even got pregnant with baby Sara."

Later in the fall of 1975, the divorce case was in full swing. The motion for temporary alimony and child support had reached the Clerk of Court and was being reviewed.

My fate lies in the hands of a judge and his clerk.

"As I've told you, this is an ugly, devious business. If we can make a decent deal, we will, but your husband's counsel wants to keep it going," Dan said. "I could draft an agreement tomorrow if they would look at it."

Legal bills were mounting for Sam. Still, Benowitz had not asked Abbie for a dime.

One late night when Sam came home, he glared at Abbie. "You should settle with me. Cut out the lawyers. That's where all the money will wind up. I can tell you this, your lawyer won't ever get a dime from my pocket."

The children were sleeping. Abbie was in her nightgown and robe cleaning up the kitchen.

Sam stood in the doorway. He was wearing a suit and a light blue shirt with a Ralph Lauren paisley tie.

"I will get custody of the children because you won't be able to support them."

"Please, Sam, let's make this divorce amicable. When we got married, we were in love. What happened?"

"I'm just not happy anymore. I have to do what's best for me."

Abbie started to cry and walked slowly to her bedroom.

Chapter Thirty-Eight

"The key to this case is getting Sam out of the house," Benowitz repeated for the umpteenth time. "That will crush him and lead the way to a settlement."

On the nights that Sam came home, Abbie found him roaming around the kitchen looking for food. He would sniff cautiously in the pots and pans of chicken and pot roast.

Abbie kept her distance to avoid arguments. At work, she told Susan, "I feel sorry for him. He looks terrible. Thin as a skeleton and has dark circles under his eyes."

"Why doesn't he work things out with you? He wants the divorce, so get it over."

"He wants me to cave. That's what Dan told me."

On her day off from teaching, Abbie sat in Dan's messy office. He was smoking one of his Parliament cigarettes and checking over brief papers that were going to be filed with the court.

He had persuaded Abbie to allege violence and beg the court for the itinerant Sam to be removed from the house. Legally, there was little chance that he would be forced out of his own house, but it was worth a try, Dan believed. There was no hard evidence of violence or injury, merely Abbie's word against Sam's. If the motion worked, it would hasten the settlement and they could get a Separation Agreement, followed by a quick fault divorce.

"What about no-fault divorce?" Abbie said. "Don't most people just figure out the finance part and get one of those?"

"A no-fault divorce sits for a year, but a divorce granted on fault could be finalized in days."

A few weeks later, Benowitz received a letter from Heller about Abbie's job. It stated, "We have ascertained that Abbie is employed as a teacher at the Irvington Elementary School."

"I'm not really shocked by that," Abbie told Susan. "This is an ugly game of slander. Slamming accusations back and forth."

"I understand if you have to quit, but you are making such a small amount of money. I don't think it will matter in the end."

She turned out to be right.

Chapter Thirty-Nine

She continued to teach three days a week and tutor some of the students after school, which demonstrated to the court that she was capable of earning money and supporting herself.

Sam was almost never around now, except technically he "lived" with them. He kept his clothes in the same closet and left his dirty underwear in the laundry for Ginger. He would drop in once or twice a week to keep an eye on Abbie and give her nasty looks.

"When are you going to come to your senses?" he yelled. "Your lawyer is using you, but he will never get a dime from me. You can't get blood out of a stone."

He certainly is not very original with his threats. Still, Abbie was scared and felt like he could strike her at any moment.

Most nights, Abbie and the kids had the house to themselves. It was such a beautiful house, although it was more formal than cozy. The living room had no TV as it was intended for entertaining. At night, after Eve and Lila finally went to sleep after sneaking back and forth like quick little bunnies between their rooms, Abbie would give a bottle to Sara about midnight, kissing the smooth dark hair on her head. It was a quiet, peaceful hour in the den, watching late-night TV while her baby drank the last ounces of her milk.

Near Christmas in 1975, Dan was expecting a decision on the Motion for Pendente Lite, the legal term for Alimony and Child Support.

Benowitz called her right before the New York Supreme Court's holiday recess.

"Abbie, there's a development. Can you go over to the train station and call me from the phone booth?"

"Is it that important? Do I really have to go to the telephone booth?"

"Yes, this is very private."

Abbie drove hurriedly to the quaint village. It was freezing with snow blanketing the ground. Her heart racing, she peeled off her woolen glove in the booth and dialed the direct line to Dan's office.

Dan picked up after one ring, and said, "Holy cow. You will not believe what Judge Santos ordered."

"What? Tell me."

"This is unbelievable. Better than I expected.

"In the judgment, Santos wrote "this legal case is going to be a contentious and protracted divorce and the Defendant must vacate the house during the proceedings."

"What does that mean? Vacate."

"It means he has to get out of the damn house…that's not all."

The judge granted Abbie temporary alimony and child support of $1000 a week until a Separation Agreement was drawn up and signed by both parties.

"This sets the tone for the entire case, sets the threshold for the amount we can ask for. Sam is going to have a run for his money."

The Order further stated that Sam had to put his clothing and belongings in boxes and vacate the house by 9 a.m. on December 31, 1975.

Abbie was shaking in the telephone booth. She noticed some acquaintances on the street. They were staring at her. She tried to compose herself.

"I can hardly believe this. How did you pull this off?" Abbie cried, swallowing tears in her throat.

"This is like a dream, in a nightmare. I don't know which."

"Good night, my darling," Benowitz said. "Be careful."

What a coup! Abbie skipped down the streets of the Village of Pleasantville and didn't care who saw her.

When Sam dropped in at the house a couple of nights later, he was thin and the circles under his eyes were darker. He yelled to the girls, "Daddy's home."

"Daddy, Daddy," cried the girls. "Did you bring us chocolates?"

I think my heart is going to break into a million pieces.

Abbie's heart ached with sadness for her broken family. The baby upstairs was sleeping. Sam went up and stood over her crib whispering her name.

Abbie walked into the room and Sam never looked at her. Then he went down to the kitchen to look in the refrigerator and pulled out the milk. "What's doing?" he said to her as she stood in the doorway. "You made a fine mess of things. I would have given you everything and now you won't get a dime."

Abbie didn't answer. She just went into her room, closed the door, and cried into her pillow. Softly, so nobody could hear.

Sometime later, Ginger, the housekeeper, gave the girls a bath and then she heard Sam leave the house and back out of the driveway.

Abbie spent New Year's holiday in Florida with the three girls at her parents' modest apartment in North Miami Beach near the ocean and an entertainment arcade. They ate out every night at the Rascal House on Collins Avenue and played games.

Her babysitter, Mrs. Birnbaum, came along to help. They slept on couches and a sofa bed.

Mrs. Birnbaum was a chubby red-haired grandmother who lived in Canarsie, a section of Brooklyn known for its tenement buildings. She often worked for a family in the city who was best friends with Rick Pollack, a divorce lawyer.

Rick's wife happened to mention to Mrs. Birnbaum that they heard about the divorce and that Sam was looking for a new attorney that might settle the case.

Sam had finally become disenchanted with Heller, the bomber lawyer.

In a letter to Benowitz, Rick Pollack wrote: "Sam Cooperman called me looking for a new lawyer. He thinks that maybe you and I can work together on a Separation Agreement."

When Benowitz told this to Abbie, she was elated.

"Does this mean we could finally end this nightmare? I feel like it will never end."

"It will end," Dan said. "It's all about the money."

Alone, though, Abbie started to worry about Pollack and Benowitz concocting a rotten deal for her.

Dan could cozy up with Rick and shortchange her, she told her mother.

"Mom am I being paranoid?"

"They could be in cahoots, but Dan has come through for you so far. I think that Sam wants this to be over, too. I just don't know why he's made it so difficult."

"He doesn't want to pay. He wants control."

Even more incredible to Abbie was that little innocent Mrs. Birnbaum knew who Sam's girlfriend was and how they met.

"*Oy vey iz mir*, you and Mr. Cooperman, such a movie star couple. He is a *meshugener*," Mrs. Birnbaum said.

Tears ran down her soft, wrinkled cheeks. "He met her on a plane. She's a Japanese lady. A businesswoman."

Chapter Forty

The grass on Abbie's front lawn kept getting drier and browner and she was about to let Ginger go, except she was afraid. Ginger might accept Sam's bribe and invent stories about her.

Three days a week, she went to her teaching job and earned about $100 a day. Susan always tried to help her out, even inviting her and the kids to her house in New Jersey.

Abbie was still waiting for the temporary alimony and child support checks stipulated by the court during the week of Christmas.

Sam called her one day. "I just want you to know, until we settle this between us, I'm not going to see the children or speak to you."

"What am I supposed to live on?"

"I don't care. Take the kids and move to Florida."

Weekly payments were due and they did not come. Benowitz filed a motion for Contempt of Court. They waited. Weeks, then months.

In mid-April, Dan got a copy of the notice from the Sheriff of New York County for Sam's arrest.

"You can put the screws to your wife, you can lie and cheat and withhold information, but you can't ignore a Court Order," Benowitz said.

The Sheriff was preparing to arrest Sam when the next day, a Certified check for 14 weeks of alimony and child support was hand delivered to the law office. It was in the amount of $14,000.

Abbie gasped, "I don't believe it."

Benowitz said, "You are going to need this money, so put it away somewhere."

After that, Sam hired a new attorney. Rick Pollack and his associate Mike Ross took the case.

"These fellows seem reasonable and sane and are going to hash out an agreement with Benowitz," Abbie told her mother.

"I'll believe it when it happens," Bessie said.

Negotiations started in earnest. Ross, in fact, insisted that Sam pay for sleepaway camp and orthodontics for the girls, if they needed to have their teeth straightened when they reached adolescence. He pointed out that it was standard in domestic agreements. They continued to argue with Dan and with their client Sam about the stipulations in the agreement.

In the summer of 1976, Sam fired Pollack and Ross. Benowitz heard that Sam thought they were too much on Abbie's side, that they were acting on her behalf.

Benowitz was not bending, "Don't worry, we will try the case in court and you will win."

In her dreams, Abbie was on the witness stand in her gray suit. Her hair was longer now, auburn, and slightly curly. She was the perfect picture of a loving mother, a Brownie leader, and a respected member of the PTA board.

In her dream she saw an exhausted Sam, his hazel eyes accentuated by black circles, was staring at her with undisguised venom. If anyone was suffering more than Abbie, it appeared to be her husband.

Then another surprise. Sam hired a new lawyer named Phillip Sweeney, a well-known matrimonial attorney with a solid reputation for settling tough cases. Dan was optimistic that he could work with him and pound out a reasonable agreement.

The thorn in the case was Sam's refusal to disclose his assets, defying the requirements of the court. Usually, a divorce settlement is based on salary, income, and assets, but there was no information available. There was only a copy of one tax return that Abbie had saved. Nevertheless, by the autumn of 1976, they became more optimistic that terms could be resolved.

But no! Sweeney used the custody card. They squeezed Abbie and threatened to file a motion for psychological examinations of the children, to determine if she was a fit mother.

She was distraught all over again. She remembered her final trip to Hong Kong when she believed that the airplane would never get off the ground.

This divorce will never end. My life is stuck.

Chapter Forty-One

Everyone was telling Abbie that there was no chance of losing custody. But there were two good women in town who had lost custody of their children. One was the mother of the twins that Lila played with. She had actually "given up" custody in a divorce suit and less than a year later, the husband had married another woman who became the stepmother.

Carole King's lyrics about not letting them take your soul reverberated in Abbie's brain. She decided to be confident about getting custody. Her litany became: I will get custody. I will have a life. The girls will live with me.

Finally, after almost two years of litigation, Dan and Sweeney hammered out an agreement. Abbie agreed to less money and had to agree to remain within 40 miles of Grand Central Terminal.

"I can't move out of state," Abbie explained to her friend Roz. "They are afraid I will move back to Chicago. I can agree to that because I have no desire to ever do that."

Finally, signatures were in place.

Abbie called her parents. "I am so relieved. The nightmare is over."

The official Separation Agreement was signed by the end of 1976, then filed in Supreme Court. On January 17, 1977, Abbie was granted a divorce by the State of New York.

Chapter Forty-Two
January 1977

After the final decree, Abbie was officially a divorced woman and a single parent. She was granted sole custody of the children, though it was less money than she had been getting under the temporary order. She received alimony and child support and Sam got a liberal visitation schedule.

Abbie told Roz, "I have to move out of the house."

"That's not fair. It's your home and the children grew up there."

"I know, but at least the divorce part is ended and I can go on with my life. The worst part of the nightmare has ended…and I have my children."

Her feelings of anxiety started to taper off, but in its place she felt rage.

She would be driving in her car and feel rage rising to the surface. She felt lost and confused about how to go forward. She had thought the battle would never end.

During the two-year struggle with lawyers and court, she had been in survival mode, with little time to feel angry. But once that was all over and legally resolved, anger rose into a conflagration.

"I feel like I'm possessed by demons," Abbie said.

"I am so mad I can't see straight," she told her mother. "Now that it's done, I'm furious."

Then a few weeks after the divorce, Sam called her. "I hope we can be friends."

She loathed Sam and Mia, the woman he was seeing. Abbie despised all the people in her life who deserted her. Only a few friends had stuck by her. Carol, her best friend, was not among the loyal.

Soon after the divorce, Carol picked a fight with Abbie and they never spoke again. Abbie guessed that it also had to do with Alan, her husband, and their own marital troubles. Their divorce came a year later.

The biggest change in Abbie's life was having to move out of her house, since it did not belong to her. The Separation Agreement stipulated that Sam give her $15,000 as a down payment to buy another house. That sum was insufficient and so he agreed to lend her an additional $10,000, making the total $25,000. At some point in the future, she would have to repay him the $10,000.

It was a meager deal, but the fighting had gone on too long. Abbie had to move on with her life. The baby, Sara, was 2, Lila 7, and Eve 8. They moved into a smaller, cozy house, on the other side of town where the houses were modest and closer together.

The neighbors were friendlier and more genuine. A few neighbors invited her over for coffee. Another neighbor included her in a car pool to get the kids to school.

"I've thought about moving," Abbie said to Dan. But since she was from Chicago, and couldn't move the kids out of state, Pleasantville was the only town where she had some roots.

"Maybe, we could move back to the city," she wrote in her diary.

I hate being a single parent, stripped of the title of "wife." Wife erased. Did he ever love me?

The money part was a struggle. She had to take the financial reins and figure out how to live on a reduced income. The alimony and child support turned out to be insufficient and she started to think about ways to make extra money. The entrepreneurial wheels in her head began to turn.

She felt unleashed and empowered to discover her talents, to cultivate dormant ambitions, such as writing.

As a catharsis, she wrote a story about her divorce and got it published in *Westchester Magazine*, which was running a feature about marriage. She wrote other articles about suburban living, school programs, and county roadways.

The divorce forced Abbie to act independently and overcome many of her old fears, such as driving into the city by herself. Sam had always insisted she wear her hair short, but now she let her hair grow long and got a perm. In spirit, she joined the women's liberation movement.

There are advantages to being alone and being a single mother, because I don't have to answer to anyone. I don't have to deal with a husband who's away half of the time. My social life can be fuller.

Gradually she began to reinvent herself. She concentrated on tennis and went to singles parties. With a new friend she met at tennis, she organized singles parties at restaurants where they met hundreds of women and men who were divorced.

To deal with her heartbreak and anger, Abbie sought professional help, going to a series of social workers and therapists, until she found a compassionate social worker who assuaged some of the pain for her and the children.

As for Benowitz, her champion, they stayed in touch for many years and saw each other several times. At age 45, he stopped smoking because he didn't feel well. Most of his time was devoted to the legal affairs of a famous Broadway producer and he even called her once from abroad to say hello.

On another occasion, Dan stopped by her house to make sure she was living comfortably. He told her that he had suffered a mild heart attack and was not his usual punchy self. She thought he was being melodramatic. They had one more romantic interlude. In the middle of lovemaking, he stopped kissing her.

"My heart, I'm having palpitations," Dan said. She didn't know if he was putting on an act or telling the truth.

Then they lost touch and about ten years later, a friend told her that he had passed away from a heart attack. That's what the announcement said in the *New York Times*. It was tragic, a great loss.

Abbie pictured him in her mind's eye, sitting at his cluttered desk, a black phone in one hand and a cigarette in the other, ashes on his cuff. Faded blonde hair, his lips smiling at her, a wink now and then. Carole King was singing, "You've Got a Friend" on a cassette player.

Dan had earned his fee, a whopping $137,000, which had been worked into the agreement. Sam had to pay it. *I'm sure he loathed that.*

Benowitz had started out helping her because her case was unique; maybe he was thinking of the money all along. She no longer questioned his motives, his acts of compassion, or his affection. Oh, yes, many times, she thought about their single tryst in the apartment, their silly romantic nights in the parking lot of the Yonkers mall, and their kisses late at night in his office, when all the other lawyers and secretaries had gone home for the night.

In my heart, I believe he loved me. More importantly, he saved me and helped me to start a new life.

Abbie wrote in her diary: *This is not going to be easy, but my life is richer now. I'm free to grow as a woman and mother, to be a good role model for my beautiful daughters. Maybe someday I will even find love again.*

Lightning Source UK Ltd.
Milton Keynes UK
UKHW010636170720
366698UK00003B/782